Welcome to
SUGARVILLE

Welcome to SUGARVILLE

A NOVEL IN STORIES BY

J.J. HAAS

LANIER PRESS

LANIER PRESS *an Imprint of BookLogix*

Alpharetta, GA

ISBN: 978-1-61005-923-7

Library of Congress Control Number: 2017918516

10 9 8 7 6 5 4 3 2   030618

Printed in the United States of America

♾This paper meets the requirements of ANSI/NISO Z39.48-1992 (Permanence of Paper)

For Melissa

The best lack all conviction, while the worst
Are full of passionate intensity.

—W. B. Yeats, "The Second Coming"

Contents

Acknowledgments

This book is dedicated to the publishing and marketing teams of Lanier Press.

Introduction

This book contains a collection of contemporary Southern short stories set in Sugarville, Georgia, a mythical town in the northeast suburbs of Atlanta. You won't find Sugarville on any map, but you will find it in the hearts and minds of the characters in this book. I affectionately refer to these characters as my Sugarvillains. They aren't really bad people at all, but lost souls searching for meaning and dignity in their lives with sometimes comic, sometimes tragic results. So let me be the first to welcome you to Sugarville, a place where the past, the present, and the future collide, and residents embark on spiritual journeys to find themselves.

About Sugarville

S ugarville, a city located in Gwinnett County in the northeast suburbs of Atlanta, Georgia, was founded in 1876 and named after the common sugar beet, a lucrative crop grown for commercial sugar production. In 1839, Evan Greysolon Ross (1798–1863), a lieutenant colonel in the US Army, led his men in the massacre of six hundred Creek Indians who refused to be relocated as required by the Indian Removal Act of 1830. When the Trail of Tears was over, Ross returned to Georgia and settled down on the land where the massacre had taken place, planting sugar beets in the same ground where he had ordered his men to bury the dead Indians. The land produced bountiful crops for many years and made him a very wealthy man. Ross eventually fought on the side of the Confederacy in the Civil War and died at the Battle of Gettysburg in 1863. The official Charter of Sugarville was approved by the Georgia General Assembly in 1876, the city bearing the name of its most famous crop.

God Helps Those
Who Help Themselves

The National Oceanic and Atmospheric Administration (NOAA) is predicting severe drought in North Georgia for the remainder of this year. Additionally, due to climate change, the possibility of "megadroughts" occurring in our region within the next decade is highly probable.

—The Gwinnett Gazette

D r. Albert Cole woke up thirsty. He must've been snoring, because his throat was sore and his wife had abandoned the bedroom like she had so many times before. He reached for the glass of water on his bedside table but, finding it empty, resigned himself to getting up and going into the bathroom. When he turned on the tap at the bathroom sink, however, nothing came out, and when he peed dark-yellow urine into the toilet bowl and flushed, the bowl wouldn't refill.

Now fully awake and annoyed, he tiptoed past the guest bedroom where Emily slept and padded downstairs in his bare feet to the kitchen. He turned on the coffee machine, but the plastic reservoir was empty, as was the filtered-water pitcher in the refrigerator. He carried the coffee reservoir over to the kitchen sink, but turning on the tap produced the same result as before. No water. He searched the pantry for bottled water and, finding none, reluctantly resolved to go to the supermarket to buy some. He walked back upstairs to tell Emily.

"Honey," he whispered, cracking open the door to the guest bedroom. "Did you pay the water bill?"

"Huh?" she said.

"The water bill."

"Uh, yeah, I think so."

"Well, the water is off in the entire house. You must've forgotten."

She sat up and rubbed her eyes. "What? I *paid* the water bill!"

"All right, all right. I'm going to go to the store to get some bottled water."

"Why?"

"Because. We. Don't. Have. Any. Water."

"Uh-huh. I'll go back to sleep."

"You do that."

He threw on a short-sleeve pullover and a pair of khakis, slipped into sockless docksiders, and hopped into his gray Mercedes convertible. The sun was already rising on Sugarville, and it looked like it was going to be another scorching summer day. He drove past the other million-dollar homes in his subdivision, exited through the gated entrance, and came out on the main road. Crossing a bridge over the Chattahoochee, he looked down to see pine trees covered in a dark-green shroud of wilted kudzu alongside a bone-dry riverbed. There seemed to be no end in sight for the drought Georgia had been suffering through for the past three years.

He pulled into the supermarket parking lot, his throat increasingly parched. A huge, black pickup truck blocked the entrance to the store, and he noticed three beefy teenagers loading cases of plastic water bottles into the truck bed. Off to the side the store manager was talking to a man in a buzz cut with a hunting rifle slung over his shoulder, the two of them presumably supervising the operation. Nobody else was there, which seemed odd for that time of the morning.

Disconcerted by the strange scene, Albert parked his car at the far end of the empty lot and watched the men from a distance for a few minutes, not knowing what to do. Finally, he decided to approach them, but not without a way to defend himself. He pulled his holstered Glock 19 out of the glove compartment and attached it to his belt, then grabbed a light jacket from the back seat, put it on to conceal the gun, and exited the car.

As he approached the store he felt surprised and relieved to recognize the man with the rifle as Earl Eubanks, someone he knew from Sugarville Baptist Church. "Hey, Earl," he called out. "What's going on?"

"Not much, Dr. C. Just buyin' a little water from my buddy here."

The store manager, a pasty-looking man in a paper-thin collared shirt, nodded at Albert and Albert nodded back. The boys continued to load the truck while the men stood in front of the entrance, effectively blocking it.

"Mind if I go in?"

"Store's closed," the manager said, stepping in front of him.

"Closed?" Albert looked at his watch. "I thought you opened at seven."

"Not today. We're waiting for a shipment."

The sliding glass doors opened with the boys carrying three cases of water each. "I don't understand. You're obviously open for Earl here. I'd like to buy some bottled water, too."

"Sorry, Mister. Earl is family."

"We're second cousins," Earl said, smiling.

"Come on, now, guys. Sell me a case of water. I'll give you twenty bucks." He pulled a crisp twenty-dollar bill out of his wallet and tried to hand it to the manager.

"No can do, Mister," the manager said.

"Well, then *you* sell me one, Earl. Here, forty bucks."

"This is for me and my family," Earl said. "You'd best be moving on, Dr. C."

"This is ridiculous!" Albert said. "My family needs water, too."

"I said no." Earl unslung his rifle in less than a second and held it out in front of him. That's when Albert remembered that Earl had once been in the military, and he backed away. "Sorry Dr. C., but if I sold you one I'd have to sell one to everybody."

Albert looked around the parking lot. "There's nobody else here, Earl."

"It's the principle of the thing."

"That's not very Christian of you."

Earl smiled. "God helps those who help themselves. Ain't that right, cousin?"

"Damn straight," the manager said.

"Like I said, Dr. C., you'd best be moving on." Earl slapped the butt of his rifle for emphasis.

"All right, all right, I'm moving," He turned around and walked back to his car in a huff.

Now thirsty and bewildered, Albert sped out of the parking lot and drove north to his favorite coffee shop, but a disembodied male voice at the drive-through said that they couldn't brew coffee without water. Driving farther north, he bypassed the speaker box at a doughnut shop and drove directly up to the drive-through window. A short, dark-skinned Indian woman in an apron said that they had plenty of doughnuts but no beverages. He mumbled "thanks for nothing" under his breath as he drove off.

As the sun rose and the heat increased, Albert experienced an acute pain at the back of his head that he attributed to dehydration. He needed to find water soon. He thought about taking off his jacket, especially because the convertible exposed him to direct sunlight, but after what had happened at the supermarket he wanted to keep his gun close, and the jacket concealed it perfectly. He kept driving north looking for some place—any place—that might have water, but most of the stores were closed, and the farther he drove the sparser the stores became until he found himself alone in the country.

And that's when his convertible started to overheat. Steam rose from the engine and poured out of the hood, blocking his view of the road. To make matters worse, he suddenly realized that in his haste to get to the store, he had left his cell phone at home. He looked around for a place to stop, but all he could find was the entrance to a park, so he turned in and found a shady spot in an empty parking lot. Once parked, Albert opened the hood and backed away from the car to allow the steam to escape.

As the steam dissipated, he realized that there might be fresh water in the windshield-washer reservoir, but he couldn't tell without removing it. He grabbed his toolbox from the trunk and, careful not to touch the engine block, pried the opaque white tank out by using a screwdriver as a fulcrum. But the tank was empty. Furious, he yanked on it with both hands, severing the rubber hose, and threw the whole mechanism into the forest.

Trying to calm himself down, he walked over to a small brick building containing bathrooms, and after checking the sinks and toilets for water and finding none, discovered an old soft-drink vending machine locked behind a steel grate. There was no place to enter a debit card and he didn't have any change, so buying something was out of the question. He considered going back to the car and getting his toolbox to try to break in, but the brass padlock looked pretty formidable, and there was no guarantee that the vending machine was stocked anyway. However, while he was standing there he noticed a boat-launch sign pointing deeper into the park and realized that he must've made it back to the Chattahoochee River. He decided to follow an unpaved road to see if he could find flowing water now that he was farther north.

Yet the answer, to his dismay, was no. The Chattahoochee was as dry here as it was near his subdivision. He couldn't remember hearing anything about the Army Corp of Engineers cutting off the water supply to the river, but devoting sixty hours a week to his cataract-surgery practice didn't leave him much time for watching the news, or anything else for that matter. In any case, he figured he was better off staying close to the river, so he followed a dirt trail going north to see if he could find a pool of water from which he could drink.

He was hardly dressed for a hike, and his sockless feet started hurting almost immediately as the path rose before him. He noticed that he wasn't sweating at all and that his headache seemed to be getting worse. As a doctor, he knew that these were bad signs, but as a dehydrated man all he could think about was getting his next drink of water and taking some back to his family. He knew that he could stop and rest at any point if he needed to, but he simply didn't have any choice but to continue.

Half an hour later he made it to the bottom of Buford Dam, but the spillway was as dry as a desert and looked like it had been that way for quite some time. A large, red "Restricted" sign sat affixed to the side of the dam and several soldiers stood on top. He knew that Lake Lanier, a huge, man-made reservoir containing the mother lode of fresh water, was directly above the dam, but he would have to climb a steep hill to get there. Fortunately, the path veered off to the right and away from the restricted area, so he continued to trudge upward, breathing heavily and cursing his docksiders.

When he finally reached the top, he couldn't believe his eyes—Lake Lanier was completely empty. The lakebed looked like a crater on the surface of Mars with an uneven pattern of dark-red mud cracks stretching out to the horizon. Old tires, beer cans, and dead fish dried by the sun dotted the alien landscape, while half a dozen vultures leisurely fed on a mutilated deer carcass nearby. He almost despaired of ever finding water again and was on the brink of uttering a prayer, but he suppressed that emotion and resigned himself to solving this problem on his own. There was nothing for it but to continue on in the direction he had chosen, so he descended the embankment and stepped out onto the lakebed to see if he could find water somewhere—anywhere.

As he searched the landscape, he thought he saw a man standing in the middle of the lakebed in the distance. Not fully trusting his eyes or even his mind at this point, he continued in the same direction and determined that it was not a mirage, but really a man—a middle-aged Native American man wearing a straw cowboy hat with two long braids hanging down over the front of his shirt. The man stood over a small puddle in the middle of the dry lakebed filling up an empty milk jug with water through a filter.

Albert quickened his pace to approach him, but by the time he got there the man had finished filling the jug and was heading in the opposite direction toward raised land. He called after him in a hoarse whisper, but the man either didn't hear or was intentionally ignoring him. He was sorely tempted to drop down to his knees and drink straight from the puddle, but the water contained animal feces that would probably give him giardia. He watched the man disappear into the brown evergreens and decided to follow him. He ran as fast as his fatigued legs would take him, climbing over a rusty grocery cart to get to the embankment and starting down the unblazed trail that the man had taken.

He reached a small, wooden cabin isolated in the heart of the forest just in time to see the man enter and close the door behind him. He hid in a clump of pine trees nearby for a few minutes, breathing heavily and trying to decide what to do. He could knock on the door and ask for a drink, but the man obviously was having trouble obtaining water too and likely wouldn't give it to him, and he simply couldn't afford a repeat of what had happened at the supermarket.

There was no margin for error and no reason for politeness—he had to have that jug. Shaking nervously, he pulled the Glock 19 out of its holster, walked up to the door, and finding it unlocked, entered the cabin with the gun raised.

The man stood at the side of the cabin next to the fireplace. "Who are you?" he demanded.

"Hands up."

The man raised his hands slightly. "What do you want? I don't have any money."

"Water," Albert said, coughing into his left hand.

"There, on the table. Help yourself."

Albert stumbled over to the table, but as he placed one foot in front of the other, time seemed to slow down, and the jug moved farther away the closer he got. He sensed his peripheral vision closing in on him like a tunnel, and he collapsed to the floor.

When he came to, he was sitting on a hard, ladder-back chair with his hands tied behind his back. The jug and the gun lay beside him on the table. The man, sitting on the chair opposite, rifled through his wallet and pulled out his driver's license.

"Dr. Albert Cole of Sugarville, Georgia. Tell me, Dr. Cole, what the fuck are you doing in my cabin?"

Albert was woozy, and it was all he could do to stay upright in the chair. "Water. I need water."

"Yes, you mentioned that. Have you ever shot anybody, Dr. Cole?"

"Um . . . no."

"Have you even had firearms training?"

"A little."

"That's obvious. Well, Dr. Cole, here's your first lesson: if you pull a gun on someone, you better be prepared to shoot them. Otherwise, you might not want to go waving handguns around. You'll just shoot yourself or provide your enemy with a weapon."

"Look, Mister—"

"*Doctor*. Dr. Robert Agaska, PhD. I teach Native American Studies at the University of Georgia."

"Oh, I see. Look, I'm sorry I pulled a gun on you, but I didn't know what else to do. If you'll just give me a drink of water, I'll be on my way and I won't bother you anymore." Albert tested his restraints. The rope was tight, but he detected a little wiggle room.

"Why should I *give* you anything? You broke into my house and pointed a gun at me." Agaska got up and walked toward the kitchen, but stopped halfway and turned around. "Do you even know where you are, Dr. Cole?"

"Lake—?"

"Wrong. You're on Muscogee Indian land."

"Muscogee? I thought this used to be a Creek Indian settlement." As he spoke, he continued to work the rope with his nimble fingers and seemed to be making some progress.

"That's the name the white man gave us, but I prefer the name we gave ourselves. I'm a descendant of the original Muscogee Indians. I was born on a reservation in Oklahoma, but I knew from an early age that this was the land of my ancestors. So when I grew up, I came to the University of Georgia to study my people and to be closer to this land. My ancestors were forcibly removed from this area in 1834 during the Trail of Tears. Surely you've heard of that?"

"I wasn't even born—"

"My ancestors didn't have a sense of personal property, Dr. Cole, but I do. So when you break into my cabin and try to steal something from me, I take that very personally. Not just for me, but on behalf of my people. To me, you're like a criminal returning to the scene of the crime."

Agaska walked into the kitchen and picked up the wall phone's receiver.

"What are you doing?" Albert said, feeling the ropes starting to loosen.

"Calling the cops."

"Don't do that! Um . . . what happened to Lake Lanier?" he asked, trying to distract Agaska from dialing. "The water seemed to disappear so suddenly."

"Maybe to you, but not to me. I've been watching Lake Lanier progressively dry up over the last three years. The short answer is that man is living out of balance with nature in defiance of the Great Spirit. He doesn't take kindly to thieves, either." Agaska started to dial.

Freeing himself, Albert stood up, grabbed the gun, and pointed it at Agaska. "Put that down."

Agaska returned the receiver to its cradle.

"Don't move."

Holding the gun in his shaky right hand, Albert took off the jug's plastic cap with his left hand and raised the container to his lips. But before he could take a sip, a gunshot rang out and the jug flew out of his hand and onto the floor. He turned to see Agaska holding his own handgun. Panicked, Albert fired wildly, emptying his

Glock 19 into the man, and watched as he crumpled to the ground.

"Goddammit!" he shouted.

He rushed over to Agaska and found him lying flat on his back on the linoleum with three bullet holes in his chest, bleeding profusely and already unconscious. He knew immediately that without a hospital nearby there was nothing he could do for the man but watch him die. He stood over Agaska crying without tears until he heard the man's death rattle and knew he was gone.

But he still needed to drink.

He found the jug lying near the front door, but between the open spout and the entrance and exit holes from the bullet, all the water had poured out onto the floor and seeped into the wood. After searching the rest of the cabin in vain, he finally returned to Agaska, kneeled down beside him, whispered "I'm sorry," and started to lap the dead man's blood off the floor.

The Greenway

After her husband died, sixty-seven-year-old Lucy Beaumont took up walking six miles a day on the Sugarville Greenway no matter what. It didn't matter if she was tired or sick, or if it was raining or snowing, she would get up at the crack of dawn every single morning of every single day and hike three miles up and three miles back because it was good for her body and good for her soul.

On this particular morning Lucy felt healthy but lonely, still missing her husband's companionship and wondering why her children had all moved so far away. She had the asphalt-paved greenway all to herself for the first part of her journey, except for a mother deer and her two fawns that vanished as soon as they saw her. It was difficult learning to live alone after forty-five years of marriage, but she was determined to stay independent in the house she and her husband had built together and resolute not to be a burden to their two adult children.

As she passed through a mist near the duck pond, she noticed a young couple from behind that physically reminded her of her parents. They were wearing street clothes instead of the workout clothes she wore, and were holding hands and whispering sweet nothings into each other's ears. As the couple sauntered down the trail in front of her in no obvious hurry, she became impatient. After all, she needed to keep her heart rate up in order to meet her cardiovascular goals. Not wanting to disturb their confidences, she slowed down her pace and walked behind them, feeling like a small child following her parents. After a while the couple left the trail by climbing a concrete stairwell to a parking lot, leaving Lucy alone once more.

A few minutes later she caught up to a man who—strangely—looked like her husband from behind. Not her elderly husband, the husband she had laid to rest the previous year, but her husband as he looked in his early twenties when they first met at the University of Georgia. He had the same short, black hair and stocky build as the man she had come to know and love as Franklin Beaumont. As she passed the young man on the left, she couldn't help but stare in wonder at his familiar facial features, which apparently embarrassed him, because he felt obliged to speak.

"Good morning," he said.

"Good morning," she floundered. "Do I *know* you?"

"Um . . . I don't think so."

She looked closer. "Franklin?"

"No, my name's Bob. Bob Sanders."

They stopped walking.

"But . . . the resemblance . . . it's *uncanny*."

"Who's *Franklin*?"

"Um . . . oh . . . never mind. I'm sorry to have bothered you."

"That's okay. Hey, are you all right?"

"Yes . . . yes, I'm fine." She started walking again and picked up the pace to put some distance between her and her embarrassment. In reality, she felt a little light headed and wondered if maybe she should cut her walk short today. But she had made herself a promise never to give up, and she was not going to give up now.

Several minutes later, the forest widened around the trail and she reached the park where she typically turned around. Dark, gray cumulus clouds with diagonal curtains of rain appeared on the horizon. The park was empty but for two small children playing with a black dog. She dreaded looking closer, but when the boy threw a ball over the trail and the dog chased after it, the children passed right in front of her. It was John and Betsy, her two young children, playing with their first dog, Blackie.

Lucy felt faint. She staggered to the trail map kiosk and leaned against it for support. She stood there for several minutes watching her children play, then started to cry as they ran off in the opposite direction and disappeared into the forest. She steadied herself and tried to read the map, but she couldn't make out the trail through her tears. No matter, her plans had changed. Instead of turning around and heading back, she looked up into the darkening sky and continued down the trail into the unknown.

Waiting for the Apocalypse

J erry Meyers marched into the CFO's office at Sugarville Financial Group promptly at 9:00 a.m. on a Monday morning and slapped his resignation letter down on the desk. A black, marble paperweight in the middle of the desk read, "It's accrual world."

"What's this?" Arnold asked, picking up the letter and studying it.

"I'm resigning."

"You're *what*? Why?"

"I'm going to start my own business."

"Just like that?" Arnold laid the letter down, loosened his tie, and gave Jerry his undivided attention.

"Well, no, I've been praying about this for a long time."

"So you're going to hang out your own shingle?" Arnold asked. "You know, a personal tax service is nothing like public account—"

"No, nothing like that," Jerry said. "It's a completely different industry."

"Well, what is it?"

"I'm not at liberty to—"

"Survival-ist-ism? Is that it? Lord knows you go on about it enough."

"Well, yes."

Arnold scowled. "What're you going to do, move your family to a log cabin in the woods?"

"No, I'm going to stay right here in Sugarville," Jerry said.

"And do what?"

"Well, if you must know, I'm going to sell prepper supplies."

"Jesus, I hope you know what you're doing, Jerry. You're one of our best accountants. Think about what you'll be giving up—your salary, your benefits, your annual bonus, for Chrissakes. You know, I can't guarantee you a position if you decide to come back. Aren't you taking this apocalypse stuff a little too seriously?"

"I *have* thought about all that, Arnold, but I'm stepping out on faith."

"Faith. Uh-huh. Can you at least stay through year-end?"

"I'm afraid not." Jerry tapped the letter with his index finger. "I'm putting in my two weeks' notice today."

"Shit. Is there anything I can do to change your mind? Sweeten the pot, maybe?"

"No, Arnold. I appreciate that, but my decision is final."

"Well, if there's no way I can convince you otherwise . . ." They stood up and shook hands. "I'll be sorry to see you go, Jerry."

***

After leading his family in a before-dinner prayer and taking a sip of sweet tea, Jerry announced, "I have some good news: I quit my job today." He took a big bite of chicken-fried steak.

Marjorie, his wife, said, "You *what*?"

"Well, you know how successful the prepper business has been. I've decided to take it to the next level."

"The next level? Without telling *me*?"

"I'm telling you now."

His ten-year-old twins, Colin and Emma, seemed to take the news in stride.

"That's great, Dad," Colin said. "It's better than being some boring CPA."

"Yeah," Emma said. "I'm always embarrassed when I have to tell the other kids what my father does for a living."

"That 'boring CPA' puts food on this table and provides us with health insurance," Marjorie said. "Well, I guess that means I'll have to go back to work." She had quit her job as an administrative assistant to take care of the children when they were small, and Jerry had insisted that she not go back.

"You won't have to do that, Marjorie. Everything will be fine. You know how careful I am with money."

"You should've talked to me first."

"The Lord has been leading me in this direction for quite some time. This is just the next logical step. Sales have increased significantly over the last six months, and now it's just a matter of establishing a network of salesmen. But I need more time to do that. I can't hold down a full-time job and work on this job at the same time. Fred made the transition from part time to full time, and so can I."

Fred Taylor was Jerry's best friend, a fellow deacon at Sugarville Baptist Church, and a prepper supplies distributor. Fred had a network of salespeople who worked for him, and though Jerry was currently just another part-time salesman, Fred had convinced him that he could make it on his own as a full-time distributor with his own coterie of subordinate salesmen.

"I'm not married to Fred!" Marjorie said.

"Now, let's all just take a deep breath and enjoy our—"

Marjorie stood up and threw her napkin down on the plate. "I lost my appetite." She marched into the bedroom and slammed the door behind her.

***

A delivery truck arrived on Saturday morning with a large shipment of prepper supplies. Jerry supervised two Mexican workers as they forklifted a dozen pallets over the lawn-preserving plywood path he had created from the driveway to the basement. His next-door neighbor, a widowed crone out walking her shih tzu, gave him the evil eye, presumably for running a business out of his house. But she hadn't said anything to him to date, and he hadn't heard a peep from the homeowners association either. In time, he hoped to rent warehouse space to store his increasingly large shipments, but he couldn't afford that part of his business plan just yet.

Jerry was double-checking the order on his tablet computer when Fred appeared at the basement door. "Howdy, stranger," Fred said. He was a tall, good-looking ex-Marine in his late forties with a perpetual tan and an easy smile who was wearing a crisp, blue blazer and a bright-red tie. "Did they get the order right?"

Jerry looked down at his tablet. "I think so. I thought some of the MREs were missing, but I found them on the pallet with the bottled water."

"Great," Fred said. "So, can we go ahead and settle accounts now?"

"Oh, sure," Jerry said, feeling rushed.

"I'm late for Donnie's baseball game."

"Oh, okay. I'll get my checkbook." He walked toward the basement stairs.

"Check, *schmeck*," Fred said. "Take a look at this puppy." He pulled out his smartphone, which had a card-swiping attachment connected to the top. "Gimme your debit card."

"My *debit card*? I don't keep that kind of money in my checking account, Fred. In fact, I was hoping for a little . . . float."

"What about a credit card?"

"Well . . . okay." Jerry reluctantly pulled out his wallet and handed Fred the credit card with the highest limit, hoping against hope that it would cover the expenditure.

Fred made short order out of swiping the card and handed it back to Jerry. "I'll send you a receipt by email. Oh, and Jerry, I'm afraid I can't make it to the party tomorrow. Debbie and I are leaving for Tybee Island right after church."

"But Fred, you promised!"

"No can do, buddy." He patted Jerry on the shoulder. "Sorry about that. You know, happy wife, happy life."

After Fred left, Jerry stood in the middle of his basement all by himself, dwarfed by the pallets containing $10,000 worth of prepper supplies that he was now responsible for selling. Feeling the weight of his decision to quit his job for the very first time, he prayed for the strength to meet this new challenge and got back to work.

***

After early church on Sunday, Jerry and Marjorie returned home to put the final touches on their prepper party. They had reached an uneasy truce whereby Jerry could pursue his dream of becoming a survival evangelist while Marjorie returned to the workforce, and they had sent Colin and Emma to their maternal grandparents' house in Dunwoody for the weekend so they could concentrate on the party. Twenty church members had RSVP'd for the big event on social media, and the preacher had even agreed to stop by to give it his blessing.

The party was supposed to kick off at 2:00, but by 2:15 only three couples had arrived, so Jerry decided to get started anyway. He led the group in an opening prayer about the end times and their responsibilities to their families, paraphrasing several key phrases from Revelation, then guided them through the displays he and Marjorie had set up in the great room.

But the response was tepid. All three couples bought a box of MREs after tasting the samples Marjorie had laid out, but they only seemed to be doing it out of politeness. None of the couples were the least bit interested in purchasing a big-ticket item like the emergency generator, and one man even had the gall to suggest he could buy something like that cheaper at a membership warehouse. Worse yet, no one expressed any interest in selling prepper supplies on a part-time basis. Net-net, that left Jerry with $9,700 worth of prepper supplies left to sell and no one to help him sell them.

As the last couple was walking out with their box of MREs, Reverend Blackwell strode up the driveway wearing the same charcoal-gray suit he had worn during the morning service. "Sorry I'm late," he said. "How did it go?"

"Well, you know, we're just getting started," Jerry said, putting a brave face on it.

Marjorie's smile melted away as soon as she closed the front door. "If you'll excuse me, I have some cleaning up to do in the kitchen."

"I want to show you something," Jerry said to Blackwell, ushering him through the house and into the backyard, where a large, blue tarp covered the ground. Jerry removed the tarp like a magician unveiling his trick, revealing a ten-by-twenty-foot hole in the red clay that was supported by a concrete floor and cinder-block walls. "You're the first person I've ever shown this to."

"Wow," Blackwell said. "What is it?"

"A bunker. I mean, it will be. It's not done yet."

"Oh, you mean like a storm shelter, for tornadoes?"

"No, no, no. This is for protecting my family from our neighbors when the shit hits the fan. Pardon my French."

"Your neighbors? Why would you need to protect yourself from your *neighbors*?"

"Because during the Great Tribulation, they'll want to steal our supplies." Jerry jumped into the hole and stood on the concrete foundation. "There's enough room in here for all four of us."

"You're planning to *live* in there?"

"Only in an emergency. Mostly it's for protecting our supplies until the militia can restore order."

Blackwell paused. "Jerry, don't you think you're taking this a little too far? I mean, I understand storing up supplies in the event of an emergency—a natural disaster, even an EMP. But if you're doing this in anticipation of the Second Coming . . . I mean, Jesus Himself said, 'But about that day or hour no one knows.'"

"Well, it's got to happen *sometime*. I don't have to tell *you* about the sorry state of the world—you preach about it every Sunday. People are getting uglier every day, evil is everywhere you look, and Satan has established a stronghold in this world. Frankly, I think we're ripe for Christ's return."

"Well, maybe." Blackwell helped Jerry out of the hole. "Look, Jerry, Marjorie came to see me the other day."

"She *did*?"

"Yes. She's worried about you. That's what I came here to talk to you about. She said you quit your job?"

"Uh-huh."

"I mean, it's none of my business, but do you think you'll be able to support your family with this new venture?"

"You're right. It's none of your business." Jerry crossed his arms.

"I mean, she was crying her eyes out, Jerry. You know what they say, men are only good for two things: sperm and income, and you already have two lovely children." Blackwell laughed, but Jerry was having none of it. "Now, Jerry, I want you to think about something for me, and I want you to keep an open mind."

"Okay. What?"

"I'd like you to consider talking to Eileen." Eileen Hayes was the Christian therapist associated with Sugarville Baptist Church. Blackwell had sent any number of church members to see her in the past, sometimes with Jerry's help, but he had never suggested it to Jerry before.

"But—"

"Now hear me out. You've been under a lot of stress lately. I think it would be a good idea for you to talk to

24

somebody, and I trust Eileen implicitly. This life change that you're going through right now affects more people than just you, you know."

Jerry's face turned red. "I'm. Not. Crazy."

"I didn't say you were. Maybe just a little . . . paranoid." Blackwell gestured to the bunker.

"Get out."

"I beg your pardon?"

"I said *get out*. You're no longer welcome here. How dare you scheme behind my back with my wife! And if you don't believe that these are the end times, then you're nothing but a hypocrite." He pushed Blackwell toward the house.

"All right, all right, I'm going," Blackwell said, stumbling up the brick staircase to the back door.

"And don't you dare tell a soul about this bunker!"

Blackwell showed himself out, and Jerry went inside to confront Marjorie about her betrayal.

***

Three months later, alone in the house, unshaven, Jerry cracked the plantation blinds and waited for the mail truck to disappear around the corner before going to get the mail. Back in the safety of his home, he rifled through the advertising mailers looking for a check, any check, but none was forthcoming. Instead, he found yet another late notice from the mortgage company and an official-looking manila envelope addressed to him.

It was the divorce papers. He knew this day was coming, but he couldn't quite believe it until he held the actual documents in his hands. Marjorie had initiated the separation two months earlier, taking Colin and Emma to live with her at her mother's house in Dunwoody, but Jerry was still holding out the hope that his business fortunes would turn around and that they could go back to living their normal lives.

But now that hope was gone. He tore up the papers and burned them in the fireplace. Retrieving his loaded rifle from the gun cabinet, he locked the back door behind him and returned to the bunker, which was now completed and fully stocked with supplies. He sat down in a camping chair in front of the bunker with the rifle resting on his thighs and, bracing himself for the conflicts to come, waited for the apocalypse.

The Cardboard Cutout

Three weeks before his sixteenth birthday, Robby Woodruff decided to play a practical joke on his parents to get them to pay attention to him. Alone in his cavernous Sugarville home after school, Robby donned a long-sleeve shirt with a collar, dug out the digital camera his parents had given him for Christmas, and prepared for a personal photo shoot in the formal family dining room. He set up the camera on a stack of schoolbooks across from his normal spot at the dinner table, switched on the self-timer, rushed to the other side of the table, and slid down into his chair. Faking a smile, he remained perfectly still as the camera automatically snapped his picture three times in a row. When he was done, he took the camera to his bedroom and downloaded the pictures to his laptop, choosing the best of the photos and cropping it until he was satisfied. He then emailed the photo to a party-supply store he'd found on the web, paying for the purchase of a life-size cardboard cutout with his secret PayPal account.

When his birthday finally arrived, Robby removed the cardboard cutout from its hiding place in his bedroom closet and surreptitiously carried it down to the dining room while his mom fixed dinner in the kitchen and his dad played with his iPhone in the den. Quietly propping up the oversized photograph against the back of his chair, Robby snuck into the foyer and hid behind the artificial Ficus tree, a good vantage point from which to watch the joke unfold.

"Marvin, Robby, time for dinner," his mom called out.

Robby's father carried his iPhone into the dining room and sat down at the table, not even bothering to look up. Robby thought his dad looked uncomfortable in the pullover and khakis he was made to wear for the occasion. Normally, he'd be in his pajamas and bathrobe by now. His dad took a sip of sweet tea, glanced at the cardboard cutout without noticing any difference, and went back to playing with his phone.

Well, Robby didn't expect much from his father anyway—he never seemed to notice Robby in the first place.

A few minutes later, Robby's mom entered the dining room with two heaping plates of food, setting the first one down in front of his dad. "Marvin, put that thing away," she said. "It's Robby's birthday." Then she placed the second plate in front of the cardboard cutout. Robby pushed the plastic leaves of the Ficus tree aside to watch her reaction, but she just seemed to be following her normal routine.

"I made your favorite," she said. "Roast beef with mashed potatoes and asparagus."

"Asparagus makes my pee smell," his father said.

"Marvin!"

She returned to the kitchen for her own plate and sat down at the far end of the table, a mile away from his father.

Robby was astonished that even his own mother didn't notice the difference. But then he had a second thought— maybe she was just playing along with the joke. That was it. He'd intended to get a big laugh from his parents and then eat his supper, but he decided to let this go on for a while longer, even though he was getting awfully hungry.

"Would you please say the blessing, Marvin?" she asked his father.

"Heavenly father, for these and your many blessings make us truly grateful. In Jesus's name, Amen." He picked up his fork.

"Marvin . . ." she said, glancing at the cardboard cutout.

"Oh, and Lord, please bless Robby on his sixteenth birthday. Amen."

"Amen," his mom said.

Robby watched as his parents started eating without him. He began to resent the cardboard cutout, which just sat there with a big, fat, fake smile on its face in its dress clothes, not saying a word, not causing a fuss, acting like the perfect son—just like Robby, only nicer.

"So, how was school today?" his father asked.

Robby almost answered from his hiding place, but then he realized that his father was talking to the cardboard cutout. Of course, the cardboard cutout couldn't answer.

"Cat got your tongue?" his father said.

"Oh, leave him alone," his mother said. "It's his special day. We'll have cake and ice cream later. And presents."

The cardboard cutout just sat there—not eating, not speaking, nothing. His mom and dad conversed on their own for a while, but then his mother noticed that Robby wasn't eating.

"Aren't you hungry tonight, dear?" she asked. No response. "Well, that's all right. You probably spoiled your dinner with your afternoon snack."

Robby was thinking this had gone on long enough, that his parents had turned the tables on him and that it was no longer funny. But his parents kept talking to that damned cardboard cutout like it was really him. What's more, they seemed to be enjoying *its* company more than they enjoyed *his*. He had to find a way to inconspicuously replace the cardboard cutout with himself.

Needing a distraction, Robby crept around to the kitchen, found the fireplace starter, and held it up to the smoke detector. The sound went off and he quickly crept back around to his hiding place, the piercing noise engulfing the house.

"*Jesus*," his father said. "You set off the damned smoke detector again!"

Robby watched as the two of them jumped up from the dining room table and ran into the kitchen. This was his big chance. He raced into the dining room, yanked the cardboard cutout from the chair, and sat in its place.

He heard his dad get up on a chair in the kitchen, pull off the cover of the smoke detector, and remove the battery. "There," he said, the noise finally subsiding.

Robby, wearing the exact same outfit as the cardboard cutout, put on the same fake smile and sat perfectly still as his parents reentered the dining room.

"Who are *you*?" his mother said.

The Waiting Room

J ack Freeman drove to the doctor's office against his will. Not only had his wife insisted he get a second opinion, but she had set the appointment for him and made it perfectly clear that she would drive him herself if he didn't promise to go. So he had promised to go, even though he knew that nothing could be done about his stage 4 brain cancer and that he would be better off accepting the inevitable than continuing to live in denial. But there simply was no point in arguing with her when she was dead wrong and adamant about it.

The waiting-room door closed behind him, sealing the fresh air out and the musty air in. The place reminded him of the inside of a coffin. It was a long and narrow corridor with black, straight-back chairs on both sides and a well-worn carpet pointing toward the reception area in the distance. The walls were unusually close together and contained amateurish paintings depicting the history of Sugarville—the Train Depot, the General Store, the First Baptist Church—but they didn't make him feel any more at home. He could hear his muffled footsteps padding down the corridor toward the light at the other end of the room.

In the middle of the room, he met two other patients seated around a circular glass coffee table. Like him, they were both older men with heads as bald as cue balls, presumably from chemotherapy. The one on the left wore half-frame reading glasses, and the one on the right sported a thick, brown mustache. Both men looked translucent in the harsh fluorescent light, and he wondered if he appeared the same way to them. Specs was concentrating intently on a tattered magazine, but Stache looked up as Jack passed and seemed surprised to see another patient.

On the wall of the reception area was a large portrait of the doctor, a genial man in his early seventies with kindly-looking eyes, all white hair, and a knowing smile that seemed to say, "Come forth and be healed." The receptionist was sealed off from the waiting room by a long line of frosted glass panels. Jack heard voices and saw movements behind the glass, but the receptionist took her sweet time sliding open a panel even after he pressed the buzzer twice.

"Next," she said, staring down at her computer screen. She was a heavyset woman in her midforties who looked like she hadn't cracked a smile in decades.

He looked around to verify that he was the only person waiting in line. "Jack Freeman," he said.

She shoved a clipboard at him. "Fill this out and let me have your driver's license and insurance card." When she was satisfied that Jack was who he said he was and that he was capable of paying his bills, she said, "Have a seat."

"How long do you think this will take?"

She looked up at him for the first time. "Do you have somewhere else to go?" The frosted glass panel slid shut with a thud. So much for Southern hospitality.

Jack walked back to the coffee table and sat down next to Specs and Stache. Specs was still studying his magazine, so he tried to start up a conversation with Stache.

"How long have you been waiting here?" he asked.

Stache looked up at the ceiling as if searching for an answer. "I can't remember," he said.

Jack had read that memory loss was a symptom of certain types of brain cancer, and since he didn't want to embarrass the man, he decided not to pursue the matter.

After a few minutes he became bored, so he picked up a coverless *Time* magazine from the coffee table and discovered it was ten years old. He had read old magazines in doctors' offices before, but this was ridiculous. He threw the magazine back down on the stack and pulled his smartphone out of his pocket, but he couldn't connect.

"They're blocked," Stache said.

"Blocked? What for?"

"I don't know."

"*Jesus.*"

He decided to play solitaire on his phone. He lost five games in a row before winning the sixth, and when he finally won he couldn't stop the microscopic cards cascading down over the screen. He tried to reboot the smartphone only to learn it had run out of battery.

He turned to Stache again. "How many people have they taken already?" He was trying not to sound impatient. After all, both of these guys were ahead of him in line.

"None," Stache said, matter-of-factly.

"I'm telling you—there *is* no doctor!" Specs said, speaking up for the first time.

"Don't start," Stache said. "You've seen the portrait."

"A portrait can be faked. That's probably an actor."

"Excuse me," Jack said. "Do you two know each other?"

"No," they replied in unison.

"So what do you want me to do?" Stache asked Specs.

"Demand to be seen!"

"I have—repeatedly. It doesn't do any good. Why don't *you* demand to be seen?"

"Because it's your responsibility as first in line."

"Wait a second," Jack said, now concerned that he wouldn't get in to see the doctor. "How long have you guys been sitting here?"

"*Forever*," Specs said, scowling at Stache.

"Well, if neither of you will demand to be seen, I will."

Jack got up and walked to the reception area, but as he reached the front desk, the receptionist locked the frosted glass panel from the inside and started turning off the lights. He rapped on the window.

"Wait a minute!"

But the lights continued going out and the voices started receding into the distance.

"What the hell!"

He ran to the interior door but it was locked as well, and banging on it proved futile.

He stomped back to Stache and Specs. "They're closing up!"

"I told you so," Specs said to Stache.

"I've never seen anything like this!" Jack said. "Are you guys just going to sit there?"

Not waiting for an answer, he marched back to the exterior door and tried the knob, but it was locked, too. He pounded on the door with both fists, then tried to force it open with the weight of his body, but he only succeeded in hurting his shoulder.

He walked back to Specs and Stache and stared them down. "What the hell is going on?"

"I think I understand," Specs said to Stache, closing his magazine and placing it on the coffee table. "He's the tiebreaker."

"The—what?" Jack said.

"That would make sense," Stache said.

Specs turned to Jack. "Tell me, friend, do you really believe there's a doctor?"

"What? Of course there's a doctor. I wouldn't have come here if there wasn't a doctor."

"*See?*" Stache said.

"Wait a second," Specs said, turning to Jack once more. "But you've never actually *seen* the doctor, have you?"

"Well, no, I guess not," Jack said.

"Then what makes you think he exists?"

"Well, I—I mean, my wife—made an appointment for me."

"So your wife made the appointment for you over the phone, and *she* probably talked to the receptionist, right?" Specs leaned in for an answer.

"I guess so. So what?"

"Neither of you spoke directly to the doctor, and neither of you has ever seen the doctor in person, have you?"

"This is absurd."

"So you have absolutely no evidence that the doctor exists," Specs said.

"If I could get in to see him, I would."

"And so would we, but neither of us has ever gotten in to see him. I just don't believe he exists."

"Of course the doctor exists," Stache said. "We just have to be patient. We'll get in eventually."

Specs sighed. "The longer we have to wait, the more ridiculous your argument becomes. But look, what if this guy really is the tiebreaker? He just seemed to appear out of nowhere. That's got to mean something."

"Maybe you're right," Stache said. "Maybe it's our job to try to convince him one way or the other. If he agrees with me, then the three of us can finally see the doctor and have the chance to be healed."

"But if he agrees with *me*," Specs said, "then the three of us can finally leave this godforsaken waiting room."

They turned to face Jack. "So what's it going to be, friend?" Specs asked. "Do you believe in the doctor or not?"

Jack didn't want to be the tiebreaker. He just wanted to confirm his worst fears and go home to die in peace with his wife by his side. But he couldn't quite bring himself to say the doctor didn't *exist*. In fact, the more he thought about it, the more he could see both points of view. Part of him would've liked to believe that this doctor might be the one who could cure his cancer, but the other part was convinced that holding out hope was a complete waste of time. However, if what these two men said was true, if the three of them couldn't go forward and couldn't go back without him choosing, he certainly couldn't make such a momentous decision in haste. He had to have more time.

"I don't know what to believe," he said, and he sat down next to the other men to begin waiting in earnest.

The Black Parade

"It starts at *nine*," Andrew Kass told his mom.

"Ten," she said. "Sit still." She stood over him at the kitchen table in her bathrobe applying white cream makeup to his face with a sponge. Dirty breakfast plates littered the table.

"*Jesus*, why don't you believe me?" Andrew exclaimed.

"Stop cursing!"

"Then hurry up. I'm going to be late."

"Did they rush Michelangelo?"

"As a matter of fact, they did."

She finished the foundation and started applying an exaggerated mouth to his face with bright-red makeup. He sat on a ladder-back chair worrying the lapels of the electric-blue vest she had made for him and tapping his oversized red-and-yellow plastic shoes on the hardwood floor.

"This would go faster if you'd stop shaking," she said.

He forced himself to sit still while she lined his eyes with thick, black eyeliner. Finally, she attached a red rubber nose to his face.

"There. Now go take a look."

He rushed over to the guest bathroom and examined himself in the mirror. Decidedly gay. But his dad had convinced him that none of his friends would recognize him once his mom was through with him, and he was probably right because Andrew could hardly recognize himself. Besides, he was going to get one hundred dollars for two hours "work" at the parade, which made getting up at this ungodly hour and pretending to be a clown all worth it. He grabbed his car keys, driver's license, and smartphone and headed out the door.

"One last thing," his mom called after him.

"What now?" he asked, exasperated.

"You have to have a name."

"No, I don't."

"I'm thinking Fallstaff. Fallstaff the Clown, with two l's."

"*What?*"

"Well, it's the Sugarville *Fall* Festival, right? So *Fall*staff, like the Shakespeare character, only with two l's. Get it?"

"Whatever," he said. Not only was his mom an English teacher, but she was an English teacher at his very own high school. And now this. Would the embarrassments never end?

"Kisses." She started to kiss him on the cheek, but thought better of it and made him bow for a peck on the crown of his orange wig.

He left the house and jumped into his hand-me-down Corolla, checking his smartphone for the time.

***

The participating groups were already lined up on the street behind the football stadium when Andrew arrived at Sugarville High School. In the distance was an imposing bank of dark, gray cumulus clouds with bad intent. He hoped the rain would hold off until after the parade, but he had a sinking feeling that it wouldn't and that his makeup would wash off, exposing his true identity.

He spotted Bob Summerour, the top salesman at his father's Ford dealership, surrounded by a coterie of teenage boys in clown regalia, none as professional-looking as his own. The only boy he recognized was Jimmy, Bob's son. Bob wore a navy-blue pinstripe suit with a loud red tie. He reeked of a sickly sweet drugstore cologne.

"Nice of you to join us," Bob said, glancing down at a clipboard. "And you are —"

"Andrew."

"Oh, *Andrew*. Of course. I didn't recognize you." He made a mark on his clipboard and set it down on the edge of a float made from paper leaves of brown, orange, red, and yellow. "Well, now that we're all here — huddle up, gentlemen." The clowns crowded around Bob as if he were a football quarterback.

"The parade route goes straight down Main Street with no turns, starting at the hospital and ending at the old cemetery. I'm going to assign each of you to a specific unit of the parade. You need to stick to your assigned unit as much as possible. Your job is simple: make the kids laugh and keep them from getting crushed by a float."

He pulled out a wad of brand-new hundred-dollar bills from his coat pocket, created a fan with the bills, and waved the fan under their big red noses. "When you're done, meet me at City Hall and I'll give you each a crisp one-hundred-dollar bill."

Andrew had never seen that much cash in one place before, but when he leaned over to get a better look, he got a noseful of Bob's cologne that made him back away in revulsion.

***

Andrew was assigned to the Sugarville Lions marching band, the last unit before the Santa Claus float, which acted as the parade's caboose and official harbinger of the holiday season. Although the football team had won only two games since Andrew had been in high school, the marching band was a vibrant organization that had won top honors at several interstate band competitions. Mr. Willis, the band director, was a former marine who expected the utmost discipline and precision from his band and strict obedience to his orders. As a result, the band looked more like a small invading army than a high school marching band, an intimidating group of two hundred seemingly single-minded teenagers in pristine blue-and-white uniforms. While he couldn't argue with the band's success, Andrew was thankful he had never learned to play a musical instrument, else his mother surely would have made him join.

The band was already standing at attention when he arrived, and Mr. Willis was reminding them to always keep their instruments up and eyes forward while they were marching. He allowed a small group of students to rush off to the bathroom before the parade started. Among that group was Amy Strickland, a perky brunette whom Andrew had asked out on dates twice before with disappointing results. She looked cute in a band uniform with her hair pulled back in a ponytail and her brown doe eyes peeking out from under a blue-feather-plumed hat. He had heard through the grapevine that she had recently broken up with her boyfriend, but he was torn between the desire to talk to her and the fear of revealing himself as a clown. However, his heart overruled his head and he followed her.

He caught the door just in time to see the band students disappearing down a long hallway to the bathrooms. A light was on in the band director's office, so while he waited he walked over to turn it off, but was surprised to find Santa Claus sitting in the band director's chair. He watched in astonishment as Santa pulled his fake white beard down over his chin, tipped a silver flask up to his lips, and took a leisurely draught. Santa seemed startled when he looked up to see Andrew watching him, but he quickly composed himself, putting his index finger to his lips and winking in co-conspiracy. Then he stood up with the aid of a walking stick that looked like a candy cane and hid the flask in one of his big red pockets. He clapped Andrew on the shoulder as he passed and said, "Ho! Ho! Ho!" with a twinkle in his eye.

The band guys emerged from the hallway first and followed Santa out of the band room; the band girls appeared shortly thereafter but raced past Andrew as if he didn't exist.

"Amy!" he blurted out, not wanting to miss his opportunity.

"Yes?" she said, looking at him like he was from another planet.

"It's me, *Andrew*."

"Andrew? Andrew *Kass*?"

"Uh-huh."

"Oh, my God! You're, you're—"

"A clown."

She laughed and turned to the other girls. "I'll be there in a minute."

Finally, they were alone.

"You look great!" she said. "Did your mom make that costume?"

"Yeah," he said, looking down at his plastic shoes in embarrassment "I'm Fallstaff. Fallstaff the Clown."

"Like the Shakespeare character?"

"Yeah, but with two l's. Wait a second, how did you—?"

"I'm in your mom's class. She's crazy for Shakespeare."

"Oh." His mom was the last thing in the world he wanted to talk about.

"Look, Andrew, I've got to get back. We're about to step off." She started walking toward the door.

"I know, I know. I just wanted to ask you . . ."

She paused. "Yes?"

"Are you planning to go to the festival concert tonight?"

"Well, maybe . . ."

"Would you . . . that is . . . would you like to meet me there?"

"Oh, I don't know . . ."

He decided to lay his cards on the table. "I heard you broke up with Tad."

"Well, there is that."

"Come on, Amy, give me a chance."

"Are you going to go dressed like *that*?"

"No. Are you going to go dressed like *that*?"

She laughed. "Of course not."

"Eight o'clock at the amphitheater?"

"All right," she said. "But I really have to go now."

"Okay. I'll see you during the parade. I'm assigned to the band."

"Great!"

He held the door open for her as she ducked her plumed hat under the doorframe, then escorted her back to her position in the clarinet section in the last row of the band. Santa sat perched on an elevated sleigh directly behind her, towering over the parade.

***

Returning to the front of the unit, Andrew witnessed a series of cascading signals that set the band in motion: Mr. Willis nodding to the drum major, the drum major marking time for the drumline, the drumline starting a marching cadence for the band members, and the band members marching forward to the cadence with their instruments at the ready like rifle-bearing soldiers poised for battle. The only one who didn't know what he was doing was Andrew himself, so he followed along behind Mr. Willis, who exuded the self-confidence of a natural-born leader in his navy-blue blazer, crisply pressed khakis, and spit-shined black shoes—a self-confidence that Andrew did not share in any way, shape, or form. In fact, the closer they got to the starting point of the parade, the more he regretted his decision to do this at all. Bob had told them generally what to do and where to go, but he had neglected to tell them anything specific about how to perform as clowns, and Andrew had the sudden realization that he was completely unprepared to do so.

As they approached the hospital where he had been born, Andrew knew the moment of performance was upon him. His heart started to race, his mouth became dry, and he began to sweat profusely. He wanted nothing more than to sit down on the curb and let the band go on without him, but he knew that would only draw more attention, not less, and he didn't want to embarrass himself in front of Amy. Besides, if he gave up now he'd never see that one-hundred-dollar bill again, and he had the ulterior motive of using it to take Amy out for something to eat after the concert. As the band members raised their instruments in preparation to play, he knew he had to think of something quick. He looked around in desperation and latched onto the solitary figure of Mr. Willis walking directly in front of him, and he had the epiphany to mimic the band director. He stood up straight, assumed an air of haughtiness, and followed Mr. Willis stride for stride just three paces behind him. The more he copied Mr. Willis's movements, the more confident he became in his role as a clown, and before long he was openly mocking the unwitting band director.

When they reached the hospital, the band started to play the fight song, and soon Andrew was in the thick of the crowd with both sides of the street lined with people. He heard a high-pitched squeal coming from his left and glanced over in time to see a little boy in a sailor suit pointing at him and laughing, which made him feel great. Unfortunately, the band's trumpeters also caught onto his mimic act and started to laugh in the middle of the fight song, causing them to flub their notes. Mr. Willis turned around and scowled at Andrew, looking like he would break him in two at any moment if he didn't cut it out. He knew he'd have to try something else. Still, getting a laugh from the little boy and the band members gave him some much-needed encouragement, and he actually started to enjoy himself.

***

At the parade's halfway point in the middle of town, the band was introduced by a diminutive local congress-man standing on a cherry picker with a microphone. "And now . . . here they come, folks! The greatest marching band in the history of the United States of America, the Sugarville High School Marching Lions! Let's hear it for them, folks. We're so glad they're here! They've been closing out this parade every year since the very beginning—even before I was born, if you can believe it— and we're always glad to have them. And behind them, you guessed it, Santa Claus!"

By this time Andrew had fully assumed the role of the clown, seeking out children in the crowd and making faces or falling down to get them to laugh, and picking up candy thrown from the floats and tossing it to them before they could run out into the street. It was exhausting and exhilarating work, but the more the children responded to him, the more satisfied he became. As he passed the emcee, he saw a little blonde girl about five years old huddling against her mother's leg, looking tired and bored. So, with his burgeoning self-confidence and a new facial expression he wanted to try out, he walked over to her, kneeled down, pulled the sides of his mouth open, stuck his tongue out, and shook his head back and forth in mock delirium. However, instead of laughing, the little girl screamed, grabbed her mother's thigh in a death grip, and started to cry.

Andrew was mortified. The girl's mother pulled her tightly against her side and said, "Oh, honey, it's just a clown!" But her laser-beam stare told Andrew it was time to move along, and that's just what he did.

***

The sky darkened, the wind picked up, the temperature dropped, and the rains finally came, just as Andrew had expected. What he hadn't expected was the intensity of the storm. Sudden sheets of water fell from the heavens, a constant barrage of cold precipitation that obscured the parade and sent the crowds scurrying into the downtown shops. Unfortunately, there was nowhere for the band to hide, so they had to take whatever the heavens allowed. Andrew was soaked to the skin in no time, his flimsy clown outfit sticking to his chest, back, and arms and his bright-orange wig turning into a lifeless mop on the top of his head. Thankfully, his makeup was still intact. Since the crowds had all but abandoned them, the band, which had continued playing the fight song off and on throughout the parade, went back to a simple cadence and trudged along in the downpour toward the old cemetery and relief, looking like a defeated army heading home in disgrace. Staring down at his shoes in a futile attempt to stay dry, Andrew quietly walked behind the band director again, the life in his step fading fast.

When he looked up between raindrops, he saw a large crowd of people rushing toward him and away from the parade's finish line. At first he thought they were paradegoers seeking the shelter of the shops, but when he saw the panic in their eyes he realized something was wrong. He asked a mother dragging her two children by the hand what was happening, but she just yelled, "Sinkhole!" over her shoulder and kept on going. He decided to break away from the band and jog toward the source of the commotion to see for himself.

Swimming upstream against an increasingly agitated crowd, he followed Main Street until it dead-ended into the old cemetery, but the old cemetery was gone. A huge, gaping hole twice the width of the street had swallowed up the wrought-iron fence and stone pillars that had once separated the cemetery from the street, and at least half of the historic graves had fallen in. Although the police hadn't secured the area yet, most of the onlookers were leaving of their own volition, but Andrew couldn't keep from inching up to the edge to get a better look. The sinkhole was an enormous, cylindrical chasm at least a hundred feet across that looked like it had been created by an angry god with a gigantic power drill. There was no telling how deep it went; he couldn't see to the bottom. Water flowed over the edge and onto the exposed red clay walls—degrading them further and making them look like they were dripping blood—and continued falling deep into the abyss, seemingly forever. The cumulative effect was that Sugarville had been blessed with its very own portal to hell.

The only other person brave enough to peek over the edge was a frumpy old crone standing under a tattered umbrella on the opposite side of the sinkhole, but when he looked up to find her a second time, she had disappeared in the rain.

Most disturbing, however, was that three-quarters of the parade units had already fallen into the abyss, and yet the parade was continuing to move forward as if the sinkhole weren't there. The next unit was the Shriners in their red mini cars making a tightly choreographed figure eight, oblivious to all that was going on around them. The befezzed old men in dark sunglasses were so low to the ground that they didn't see the impending drop-off, and their mini cars made such a loud buzzing noise that they couldn't hear the few remaining people shouting for them to stop. Andrew wanted to run out into the street to prevent them from going over, but they were driving so fast he was afraid he would get hit, or worse yet, fall over the edge himself, so he stood there paralyzed on the sidelines watching in horror as every last one of them drove into the chasm.

Rattled, he set his sights on warning the next unit, a jet-black Mustang convertible with a Sugarville Ford sign on the door. Inside was Bob Summerour being driven by his son Jimmy, still in his clown costume. They were both drenched, but Bob continued to sit on top of the muscle car's rear-seat frame, smiling and waving to the nonexistent crowd. Revived by fear, Andrew ran out into the middle of the street, held up his hands in front of the car, and yelled, "Stop!" at the top of his lungs. The Mustang pulled up just short of hitting him, and when it came to a complete stop, he ran around to the side to warn Bob.

"What the fuck are you doing?" Bob said. "I have to get this car in out of the rain."

"There's—there's—"

"Spit it out, son! Are you a clown or a mime?"

"A sinkhole! There's a sinkhole! You've got to stop!"

"*What?* This is the most expensive car in the showroom, and it's getting *completely soaked.* Step on it, Jimmy!"

Jimmy hit the gas, and father and son plunged headlong into the sinkhole. Andrew ran up to the edge to see Bob's wad of one-hundred-dollar bills fluttering to the bottom of the chasm like a colony of bats returning to a cave.

He stood stunned for several seconds until he realized the very next unit was the band, which was marching lockstep toward the sinkhole with their instruments in front of their faces, blocking their view. His thoughts immediately turned to Amy and how he could save her from this madness. He'd had his fill of so-called authority figures, so he bypassed Mr. Willis and ran straight to the back of the band, where Amy was still diligently marching in time with the relentless cadence.

"Amy, you've got to come with me right now!"

"*What?*"

The first row of the band reached the edge of the sinkhole and toppled over like toy soldiers falling off the end of a conveyor belt.

"Come with me—now!"

"I'm marching, Andrew. I have to finish this parade."

He grabbed her by the arm and tried to pull her out of formation, but she ripped her arm away and glared at him.

"*Jesus*, why don't you believe me?" he shouted.

Exasperated but refusing to take no for an answer, he scooped her up in his arms like a groom carrying his bride over the threshold, now determined to forcibly remove her to the safety of the sidewalk. Amy flailed in his arms and cried out for help. Ever the hero, Santa jumped from his float and ran over to the commotion. In an instant, Andrew felt a sharp *THWAP!* on the back of his head that made him drop Amy to the pavement, and the last thing he saw before passing out was Santa's candy-cane cane coming down on his forehead.

Regaining consciousness a few seconds later, he looked up to see the last three rows of the band approaching the sinkhole. He stumbled to his feet and tried to reach Amy before it was too late, but he was too dizzy to run and could only watch in disbelief as she marched into the chasm along with everyone else. He walked as fast as he could to the sinkhole and looked down, but by the time he arrived she had disappeared into the abyss. He stood at the edge with tears streaming down his face and his arms outstretched in supplication, bereft.

From out of nowhere, the frumpy old crone walked up to him, held the tattered umbrella over his head, and said, "Wasn't it wonderful?"

The Disappearing Man

*My formula for greatness in a human being is
amor fati: that one wants nothing to be different,
not forward, not backward, not in all eternity. Not
merely bear what is necessary, still less conceal it—
all idealism is mendacity in the face of what is
necessary—but* love *it.*

—Friedrich Nietzsche

After his wife left him for another woman, Tom Faria
found himself frequenting the gym on a regular basis,
not out of some idealistic notion about getting into shape,
though that was one of the consequences, but more to
provide himself with a reason to get out of bed in the
morning. This morning, after thirty minutes on an elliptical
machine and another thirty minutes of strength training, he
headed for the showers, closing his eyes and letting the
almost painful streams of hot water cascade down over his
forty-four-year-old body. Still half asleep, he pumped
liquid bath soap into his palms and lathered up his hairy
chest, but when he reached his legs he noticed his feet were
missing.

At first he thought his eyes were playing tricks on him—
maybe he'd accidentally rubbed soap into them or couldn't
see straight without his contacts—but as he continued to
stare, he came to the inescapable conclusion that both feet
were completely invisible from the ankles down. He could
still *feel* them, and in fact he was still standing on them, but
he could no longer *see* them. Suddenly light headed, he

leaned against the tiled shower wall for support, then closed his eyes and took several deep breaths to steady himself. Yet when he opened his eyes again, his feet were nowhere to be seen.

Well, he couldn't stay in the shower forever. Turning off the water and wrapping a towel around his waist, he walked briskly to the locker room, located his gym bag, and immediately put his socks on. Luckily, the place was empty, so there was no one there to witness his personal embarrassment. But now he had a dilemma: should he drive into work as planned, or go back home and make an appointment with his doctor, or maybe even his therapist? He finished dressing and sat on the wooden bench for a few minutes weighing his options, then decided to go into work anyway because he was expected at a mandatory reorganization meeting, and his missing feet were safely hidden behind business casual attire.

***

The conference room at Sugarville Software was packed with programmers eager to learn their fate. Tom arrived last and had to sit in a broken chair next to his manager, Frank Winslow, who sat at the head of the table. Marsha Devereaux, the only other project leader besides Tom who reported to Frank, sat directly opposite him but a foot and a half taller because Tom found it impossible to adjust the height of his chair.

"So good of you to join us," Frank said, looking down on Tom with piercing brown eyes and unnaturally black hair. Frank was a seasoned numbers guy who didn't know the first thing about developing software. He'd been brought in from the outside by the CIO six months earlier. So far he'd allowed Tom and Marsha to run their teams as they always had, but everyone knew this was his first opportunity to put his stamp on the department, and the anxiety was palpable.

"Good morning, everyone," Frank said. "First, I want to assure everyone that layoffs will *not* be a part of this reorganization. I didn't bring you into the office today to hand out pink slips. In fact, I have some very good news. I know that many of you have heard the scuttlebutt about us developing a new application, code-named Phoenix, and I wanted to let you know that upper management has approved that project."

Several people clapped spontaneously, helping to ease the tension. Tom had worked nights and weekends on a proof of concept for the Phoenix project and was quietly pleased that his vision for the application had been vindicated.

"However, I've decided to reorganize the department to make the best use of our resources. Starting today, I'm combining Marsha's and Tom's project teams into one development organization. I'm appointing Marsha to the new position of product manager, reporting to me, and I'm assigning Tom to the new role of system architect, reporting to Marsha. Marsha will be responsible for managing the department on a day-to-day basis. Tom's new role will allow him to concentrate on the technical details of the software, freeing him up from the responsibilities of supervising people. Those of you who used to report to Tom will now report to Marsha going forward."

Although the reorganization was met with general approval, Tom felt blindsided by the change and angry that Frank hadn't discussed it with him before announcing it to the entire department. Effectively, he was being demoted.

He somehow managed to conceal his surprise while offering his hearty congratulations to Marsha, but beneath the table his feet began to itch. He reached down to scratch them surreptitiously as the celebration continued around him, but he couldn't seem to get any relief, and soon they felt like they were on fire. He had to find some relief and soon. Waiting until Frank moved onto the next agenda item, Tom quietly slipped out of the conference room and headed for the bathroom.

Locking the stall door behind him, he yanked off his shoes and scratched his feet through the socks until he was completely satisfied. However, as he pulled his pants legs up to reach his calves, he saw that both of his legs were now invisible from the knee down. He sat on the toilet seat for a few minutes waiting for a bout of nausea to pass, then put his shoes back on and left for the day without telling a soul.

***

Back at his apartment, Tom quickly undressed and examined himself in a full-length mirror. Not only were his legs invisible from the knee down, but he could actually see them disappearing up his thighs at a slow but steady rate. He paced back and forth in the bedroom wondering what to do, and finally decided to call his therapist, who'd been treating him for depression ever since the divorce. He felt they'd developed a good rapport and he could trust her with any problem, but how she'd react to a delusion of this magnitude was anybody's guess.

When he dialed her direct number, however, he got a voicemail reminding him that she was on vacation this week. She provided a forwarding number for another therapist in her practice, but it had taken him a monumental effort to even call her the first time, and he simply didn't feel comfortable discussing this problem with a complete stranger. Fortunately, she had prescribed Xanax for anxiety, so he took a double dose and eventually fell asleep on top of his unmade bed.

***

He awoke to an incessant pounding on his front door. Still naked, he threw on a pair of blue flannel pajamas, covered up his legs with long, white tube socks, and peered through the peephole. It was Kecia, his personal trainer, holding several bags of groceries. *Holy shit*, he thought. They'd only been dating a month, but the last time he slept over at her place he'd promised to let her come to his place the next time. Apparently, this was the next time. He opened the door.

"Are you all right?" she said. "I rang the doorbell."

"Um . . . yes, I'm fine. I must've fallen asleep. What time is it?"

"Six o'clock. Aren't you going to invite me in?"

"Oh, yeah, sure. Sorry." He kissed her on the lips and took the groceries.

Kecia was a light-skinned black girl in her midtwenties who looked great in spandex, but tonight she was wearing a low-cut red top, tight designer jeans, and black boots that made her even more desirable. In fact, so far their entire relationship revolved around sex, which for him was a breath of fresh air after the painful end of a joyless marriage. But sometimes he suspected that she saw lovemaking as just another aerobic exercise, a way to get the endorphins flowing, and he half expected her to require him to start wearing a heart monitor. He certainly didn't feel like entertaining tonight, let alone pushing his body to the extremes she typically expected, but he couldn't think of a good way to get rid of her. The truth, of course, wasn't an option.

"Why are you in your pajamas? Didn't you go into work today?"

"Well, I did, but I came home early. I wasn't feeling well."

"What's the matter?"

"Nothing. Just a headache."

"If I stayed home every time I had a headache, I'd never go to work." She seemed right at home in his kitchen as she started unpacking the groceries. "You just sit down on the couch and relax. I'll fix dinner. You can even stay in your PJs."

She opened a bottle of pinot noir and handed him a glass, and soon the apartment was filled with the rich aroma of broiled salmon. He tried to play a first-person shooter on his gaming console in the den, but he was too groggy to aim and too nervous to concentrate, worrying all the while that she would insist on playing with *his* joystick later on, not knowing if there was anything down there for her to play with.

After dinner, they returned to the couch with a second bottle of wine, ostensibly to watch the Braves game, but soon found themselves entwined in a passionate French kiss. However, when she placed her hand on his thigh, he suddenly froze up.

"What's wrong?"

"I don't know. I'm a little anxious tonight."

"Just tonight? You're the most high-strung person I've ever met. That's why I'm good for you. I help you relax."

She returned her hand to his thigh and gradually moved it up to his crotch.

"I have an idea," he said, hatching a spontaneous plan to save himself.

"Me too." She smiled.

"Let's go to bed."

"I thought you'd never ask."

Closing the door behind them, he proceeded to turn out all the lights in the bedroom until it was pitch black. They met in the middle of the bed, undressing each other by touch, and made love like shadows in the dark.

***

In the morning, realizing he was still naked and the sun was rising, Tom grabbed his pajamas and socks and tiptoed to the bathroom so he could get dressed before Kecia woke up. But when he turned on the light and looked in the mirror, he realized that now his entire body was invisible, and that clothes would no longer conceal his condition. He stood there for several minutes staring at the mirror in disbelief, but it wasn't long before he heard Kecia moving around in the bedroom. With nowhere to hide, he panicked, rushing around the bathroom like a rat trapped in a maze until he blacked out.

When he regained consciousness, Kecia was kneeling down beside him. "Tom! Are you all right?" She helped him sit up and lean back against the cold porcelain bathtub.

"You . . . you can see me?"

"Of course I can see you. Bless your heart, you're delirious."

After a few minutes, she helped him stand up and led him back to the bed, propping his head up with a pillow and tucking him in. As he looked up at this angel of mercy nursing him back to health, he finally understood that he was only invisible to himself, not to other people, and he vowed then and there to keep his affliction secret for fear of being considered crazy. Although his invisibility was beyond his control, his emotional reaction to it was entirely up to him, and perhaps with time he could accept or even embrace his fate.

Besides, maybe everyone was invisible.

The Package

The package must have arrived during the night because it was resting on Jacob Osbourne's welcome mat early in the morning. The lightest of sleepers, Jacob was up with the sun and spotted the small box wrapped in coarse, brown paper sitting on his front porch. He twisted his head to get a better look through the front-door window, but all he saw was the thick string holding the package together.

He didn't know what to do.

After ten minutes of indecision, he went to the garage and grabbed his extended pruning shears, then put on his Kevlar vest and gloves. Turning off the security alarm and unlocking three deadbolts, he cracked the front door and peeked out.

So far so good.

Standing back from the door, he angled the pruning shears through the opening and nudged the package with the tip, then nudged it a little farther. When he had pushed the package several inches without incident, he was relieved. At least temporarily.

Now he had to pick the damned thing up.

Setting the shears down in the foyer, Jacob opened the front door wider, stuck his head through the opening, and looked down at the package. His name and location were correct, but there was no return address. He knew it was risky, but before he could stop himself he swung the door wide open and picked up the package.

To his amazement, nothing happened.

Gaining confidence, he carried the package into the kitchen and set it down on the island. He carefully removed the string, slowly unwrapped the package, and pulled the paper away from a slick, white box. Written prominently on top of the box was the name of a familiar company.

Thank God, it was only his medicine.

Soulmates

Katie never bothered dressing before noon. She was makeupless in her pink PJs with her shoulder-length brown hair tied back in a bun. After making a quick breakfast for Mason and the kids, wrapping them up like birthday presents in the SUV and kissing them all goodbye, she carried her decaf vanilla latte into the home office and prepared to start her day.

The home office was Katie's refuge from the petty intrusions of the everyday world. In it were her desk and computer equipment, overstuffed bookshelves, a comfy blue couch, and the virtual-reality lounge provided by Virtual Escorts. But what she really liked about her office was the peace of mind it afforded her, and the privacy. It was the one place left in the world where she could still hear herself think.

She set the coffee on the desk, booted up her laptop in its docking station, and checked her email. A message from the agency warned of yet another computer virus infecting the network. But there really wasn't anything Katie could do about it—she just had to trust that the techno-geeks back at the office would handle it so she could concentrate on her job. She deleted the email along with several others, powered on the VR lounge, and got ready for her eight o'clock.

The lounge was a comfortable black-leather chaise with a simple VR cable attached to the back. The agency had it delivered to her house very discreetly three months earlier.

Before that, Katie had to drive to midtown Atlanta on a daily basis, a commute that could take her up to an hour and a half each way. But then upper management had instituted a progressive telecommuting policy, and Katie was allowed to work from home as a reward for being a top-performing consultant. Anyway, it really didn't matter where Katie worked physically—she had clients all over the world.

Ten minutes before her scheduled engagement, she turned off her cell phone, lay back in the lounge, and plugged the VR cable into a port embedded in her temple.

***

Katie felt a familiar rush of excitement as she materialized as a voluptuous redhead. She stood naked before an ornate, gold-framed mirror in the empty parlor of an eighteenth-century French chateau. She smiled to herself as she examined her cascading curls, full, freckled breasts, and fiery red bush. Perfect, as usual.

"Black lace panties with a push-up bra," she said, and the program responded by covering her up.

She knew most of her colleagues configured their avatars before entering VR, but dressing in the program actually helped her to get in the mood. And, God knew, she needed all the help she could get at eight o'clock in the morning. Besides, she suspected it was her meticulous attention to detail that made the virtual world seem so realistic to her clients, and led to a long list of repeat customers.

"Okay, let's shoot for something sexy but conservative."

A black pinstripe suit suddenly enclosed her body like a Chinese finger trap.

"Too . . . tight. And way too conservative. Maybe a dress."

The suit was immediately replaced by a black evening gown that accentuated her auburn hair.

"Better. Now raise the hemline above the knee."

She turned in a circle and admired herself in the mirror.

"Okay, but make it sleeveless with a plunging neckline. Good. Add black sandals. Okay, now the makeup."

Her features blossomed with expertly applied eyeliner, eye shadow, and rouge. Her pouty lips came to life with provocative red lipstick.

"Now the jewelry. Diamond stud earrings, with a matching necklace."

The program responded with a graceful platinum diamond necklace set.

"Perfect," she said.

The transformation was complete. Katie had become the woman she had secretly desired to be ever since she was a teenager.

She had become Veronica.

***

The porcelain mantel clock read 7:58 a.m. as Veronica walked through the Louis XIV furniture past the spacious bedroom and opened the French doors to the balcony. Seabirds patrolled the Mediterranean shore, and a gentle summer breeze blew the billowy cream sheers back into the parlor.

On the balcony was a small, circular table covered with a white linen tablecloth and spread with elegant china, silverware, and crystal. In the middle of the table was a delicate Chinese lantern hand-painted with tiny white-and-green flowers and flowing black calligraphy. A Mozart piano concerto played somewhere in the background.

As the sun began to set in the west, Veronica sat down in one of the chairs, lit the lantern programmatically, and took a sip of Veuve Clicquot.

The empty chair opposite her shimmered as a human form started to occupy it. Pixels like gnats congregated in the trunk and danced their way outward to the head and arms. Soon the ethereal shape solidified and Veronica recognized the person behind the shape as her first client, Angie.

"Good evening," Veronica said.

"Good morning," Angie replied, and they both laughed.

"I had a perfectly awful day, Vee. I'm telling you, those Chinese bastards might as well repeal the Basic Law. I'm starting to regret moving my company to Hong Kong in the first place."

"Oh, you know you couldn't live without it," Veronica said. "The power, the prestige. You're leading an exciting life, Angie."

"Yeah, but it's getting damned hard to run a software company there."

Angie's avatar was a smart-looking businesswoman in a two-piece suit with cropped blonde hair and a masculine jawline. Although her clothing changed from meeting to meeting, her physical appearance remained the same, and she always managed to look as if she had just come from the executive boardroom. With the myriad of possible identities Angie could have adopted, Veronica thought it unusual that she chose to be the same person every week.

What's more, Angie insisted that Veronica continue to appear exactly as she had during their very first encounter.

Angie smiled and visibly tried to relax. "Anyway, I didn't come here to talk business." Her eyes roamed over Veronica. "You look absolutely stunning."

"Thanks," Veronica said.

Angie raised her glass. "Let's have a toast. To our anniversary."

They clinked glasses and sipped champagne.

"I didn't realize that you were . . . keeping track," Veronica said.

"Six months to the day. You know how much I enjoy our little liaisons."

In real life, Katie had never made love to a woman and didn't remotely consider herself a lesbian. But after dozens of the same-old-same-old one-night stands in VR, she had jumped at the chance to try something different when the agency offered her the opportunity. As Veronica, she had let her imagination run wild during her first lesbian encounter. When the customer-satisfaction survey came back positively ecstatic, the agency started sending the bulk of their lesbian clients her way.

"What's for dinner?" Angie asked.

"I was kind of leaning toward the duck *à l'orange*."

"Not tonight, Vee. We need something special for our anniversary. Something . . . romantic." She thought for a moment. "I know. Chateaubriand."

Angie clapped her hands, and two dinner plates with silver covers appeared before them. She reached across the table and removed Veronica's cover with a flourish.

Beneath it were three heavy slices of beef with new potatoes and asparagus.

"That's what I love about VR," Angie said as she lifted her own cover. "You can eat whatever you want with absolutely no consequences."

Veronica cringed silently as she thought about pairing beef with champagne, but she bit her tongue and reminded herself that the customer was always right.

***

Katie had originally taken the job at Virtual Escorts as a stopgap measure after Mason was laid off and out of work for several months. At first, he had been openly skeptical of her "part-time job," but she was convinced there was no alternative because their finances were in shambles. Without Katie's job, they certainly would have lost the house and may well have had to declare bankruptcy.

Mason finally had found another job, but it was a big step down from his lucrative and prestigious former position. Ironically, not only did his new job provide significantly less money, but Mason also had to work longer hours, and rarely came home before Katie had already put the kids to bed. She saw very little of him these days, and when she did, he was tired and resentful.

By the time Mason had found his new job, Katie had been at the agency for over three months. She'd made the transition from part time to full time. She had also gone from the exclusively male clients that Mason found so objectionable to the female clients he was more willing to accept. Anyway, he never seemed to complain when Katie recounted her affairs with women while they were in bed. But Katie made a point of never mentioning Angie to

Mason. She somehow felt it would be a betrayal of Angie's trust.

Now—as the money poured in like a waterfall and she embraced the creativity of her job—Katie found it increasingly difficult to quit. Thus, she and Mason told the kids and their close friends that she was a technical writer documenting a new VR technology, and she kept right on working. Besides, as Mason always said, it wasn't like she was a prostitute or anything—the entire job was just a figment of her imagination. As long as she was able to maintain a clear dividing line between fantasy and reality, Katie would be just fine.

***

With dinner over and the chocolate mousse just a pleasant memory, Veronica and Angie sat sipping the dregs of their sweet red dessert wine. Angie had shed her jacket, revealing pert little breasts beneath a sheer white blouse and lacy bra. Although Veronica was starting to feel a little tipsy, she knew precisely how much alcohol she could handle, and was confident that her inebriation would fade as soon as she left VR.

"You know, Vee," Angie began, "I've told you so much about myself, but I know so little about you."

"I don't like talking about my personal life," Veronica said. "Besides, the agency doesn't allow it."

"The agency, the agency. You're always hiding behind the agency. Still, I find myself wondering who you really are. I mean, are you a businesswoman like me? Or a prostitute who found a safer way to make money? I'd like to think you're an artist of some kind—I guess it's just the romantic in me."

Veronica responded with silence. Lately Angie had been getting awfully possessive, making her feel more and more uncomfortable each week. She was having to work harder and harder just to deflect these questions, and she felt torn between her desire to please Angie and the need to protect her privacy. But there was something more: she was starting to wonder if she had genuine feelings for Angie.

"I sure hope you're not a man," Angie said.

"I told you before—that's against the rules."

"Yeah, but you wouldn't be the first person to lie in cyberspace."

"I'm not lying, Angie. The agency won't let a man pose as a woman, or vice versa. They have strict guidelines about these things, and they monitor them very closely. Clients can be whatever they want, but consultants have to be the same sex as they are in real life."

"Well, I already told you I'm a woman."

"You didn't have to do that."

"I know, but I wanted to. Jeez, you sure have a lot of rules you have to follow. I only have one rule: it's easier to beg forgiveness than to ask permission."

Angie laughed, but Veronica was feeling a little defensive.

"The rules are there to protect us, Angie—and our clients." She wasn't sure whom she was trying to convince, Angie or herself.

"Do you think you need to be protected from me?"

"Of course not. But you're not my only client. Most of my clients are men posing as women."

"Really? How do you know that?"

"Well, I don't know for sure. The agency guards their true identities. But it's pretty self-evident in the bedroom."

"Oh, I see. They can get a little rough?"

"You could say that. And most men wouldn't spend five minutes on a romantic dinner like this."

They both laughed.

"Those men just don't know what they're missing," Angie said. "The anticipation is half the fun." She then got up and started massaging Veronica's shoulders from behind, and Veronica could feel the tension in her body melt away.

"I bet your *boyfriends* don't do this," Angie said.

"No . . . they don't," Veronica purred.

Angie leaned over Veronica's shoulder and whispered in her ear. "I don't mean to pry, Vee. It's just that I get so lonely all by myself in Hong Kong. You're the only person I see, socially."

"But you go out to the clubs all the time," Veronica said.

"That's just business. There's no such thing as a personal life for an expat in Hong Kong. You do your first job from nine to six, and your second job from six to midnight. I spend most of my time entertaining clients. Talk about prostituting yourself."

Angie helped Veronica to her feet and kissed her full on the lips. Veronica felt a tingling sensation coursing through her body like electricity.

"So, am I really the only woman you see?"

"Yes, Angie. As far as I know, you're the only one."

Angie smiled. "Good." She took Veronica's hand and led her into the bedroom.

***

It was a large and luxurious bedroom with a king-size bed, matching armoire and nightstands, two overstuffed chairs, and a rollback chaise. Several Monet landscapes hung serenely from the rich, brocaded wallpaper. Knotted at the top of the carved mahogany headboard was a sheer cream-and-gold canopy that flowed down over the bed like a gently rippling stream.

Veronica removed the multiple stacked shams and satin pillows, and turned down the quilted silk bedspread. Angie approached her from behind and slowly started unzipping her dress, tenderly kissing every inch of her immaculate skin from the nape of her neck to the small of her back. Before long they were both lying naked on the bed.

"I have a surprise for you," Angie said, propped up in the bed on one elbow.

"What kind of surprise?"

"It's an anniversary gift."

"But I didn't get you anything."

"That's all right. This is for both of us." Angie leaned over and initiated a long French kiss.

Veronica smiled. "Was that your surprise?"

"Not yet. Close your eyes."

"*Angie.*"

"Close them, and keep them closed."

Angie reached over and held both of her hands as Veronica closed her eyes.

Suddenly, Veronica felt the room spinning around her, twirling in paroxysms of motion. She knew she wasn't drunk, so this had to be something else. Instinctively, she tried to open her eyes but couldn't do it, and she felt herself starting to panic.

"What's going on?" she said.

"No peeking," Angie replied.

The spinning gave way to the feeling of forward movement, followed by the unsettling sensation of hurtling through space at a tremendous rate. After a few seconds, Veronica felt herself being pulled inexorably downward into a spiraling whirlpool, then falling weightlessly into a limitless abyss. She felt like she was going to be sick.

"What's . . . happening?" she managed to say.

"You'll see. Just hold on."

Veronica gripped Angie's hands with all her might.

Finally, after what seemed like an eternity, Veronica's free fall slowed appreciably, then came to an abrupt halt. Her nausea was dissipating, but she felt disoriented and was having difficulty getting her bearings. Although Angie was still holding onto her hands, Veronica could sense they were no longer lying next to each other on the bed. Instead, Veronica felt like she was lying down with Angie standing above her.

"Open your eyes," Angie said.

Veronica looked up and saw Angie smiling down at her.

"Where . . . where are we?"

"Take a look."

She examined her surroundings and realized she was back in her home office, lying down on the VR lounge. Everything was exactly as she had left it.

"What did you do?" she asked, too confused to be angry.

"I wanted to meet you, so I planted a little program on the agency's server. They really need to upgrade their firewall."

"You? The virus?"

"Well, technically I guess you could call it a virus. But I'm not planning to do any mischief—I just wanted to meet you in person. You're very pretty."

Veronica looked down at her pink PJs and suddenly realized she was back to being Katie. Feeling naked and vulnerable, she let go of Angie's hands and crossed her arms over her chest.

"Oh my God!" she said.

"It's okay, sweetie. I'm not going to hurt you."

"How did you do this?" she demanded.

"Well, it's complicated. Suffice it to say that we're still in VR, but we're projecting our default avatars instead of our role-playing avatars. And I customized the location based on your residual memory."

"Default avatars? But you look exactly the same."

"That's because I'm a holistic—the same in VR as I am in real life. I think it's dangerous to pretend to be somebody you're not, so I never assume a role-playing avatar. And I don't think you should either . . . Katie. That is your real name, isn't it?"

"Yes, but how do you know that?"

"I don't think it's good for you to maintain a fragmented personality for such a long time. It's bound to have serious psychological consequences. I've been worried about you over the past couple of months. You can't go on living a lie."

"Living a lie?" Katie said defensively. But the more she thought about it, the more she realized that Angie was right. She looked away for a moment and noticed an old photograph of her with Mason and the kids at the beach. It seemed so far away, so distant, so removed from the person she had become. If Katie really was living a lie, she no longer could tell which of her two personalities was the truth.

"Maybe you're right," she said.

Angie caressed Katie's cheek. "It's okay. It's never too late to make some adjustments."

"But how?"

"Well, you can start by being honest with yourself." Angie paused to take a deep breath, and then exhaled slowly. "And then you can try being honest with me."

"Honest with you?"

"About your true feelings."

"What do you mean, 'my true feelings'?" But Katie knew exactly what she meant.

"Okay," Angie said, "I'll go first. I'm in love with you, Katie. Not with Veronica, not with some idealistic notion of who you are, but with you."

Katie was stunned. Angie's simple declaration completely obliterated her façade. In an instant, all her rationalizations evaporated and the secret she'd been keeping from herself came flooding out.

"I love you, too," she said.

And with that, Katie could feel her world—her real world—come crashing down around her.

A Model Citizen

For Jeddy

M artin Eldridge woke before dawn on his seventy-fifth birthday eager to initiate his secret plan to have the identity chip removed from his brain. He knew his wife, Valerie, never would have approved, but Valerie had died from pancreatic cancer the previous year and no longer had a say in the matter. He missed her terribly, but he felt he had more than fulfilled his obligations to society and, absent the constraints of a wife and family, wanted only one thing for himself: freedom.

He ate a lonely breakfast of cold cereal at the kitchen table in his Sugarville home and watched the news on TV. President Trumbull announced that the United States was annexing Liechtenstein from the European Union. Martin thought, *What in the world could the United States possibly want with Liechtenstein?* But there it was. The tiniest country in Europe would become the sixty-third state after Mexico and Australia, and true to form, the Liechtensteiners would be selectively sterilized and implanted with identity chips.

Martin had received his own identity chip twenty years earlier, right after Trumbull declared himself President for Life. At that point, he still had a family to support, so he felt compelled to submit to the procedure to keep his job as an air-traffic controller with the FAA. He never felt comfortable knowing that a microchip was embedded in his brain—in fact, he had always considered it an invasion of his privacy—but of course he could never complain about it. Not only did the chip make all his personal information readily available to the government, but it contained a GPS tracking device that pinpointed his every move twenty-four hours a day, seven days a week. Trumbull had said he was instituting the mandatory domestic program for "the protection of all Americans," but everyone knew it was just his way of controlling the population and rooting out subversive elements.

After a quick shave and shower, Martin got dressed and combed what was left of his hair over the bald spot in front. He took his lucky penny out of its hiding place in a chest of drawers and placed it in a small, leather change purse, which he stuck in his right front pants pocket next to a magnet he'd bought at the grocery store. Then he went to the garage and cranked up his ancient blue Buick, which he'd loaded with luggage the night before.

Driving south on I-85 to downtown Atlanta, he got off at Spring Street and parked near the Russell Federal Building. Once inside, he passed through a metal detector, took the elevator up to the third floor, and followed a long corridor to an office with a sign that read, "United States Department of Homeland Security, Identity Clinic."

It was only eight o'clock in the morning, but the waiting room was already packed. Dozens of patients from all walks of life were waiting to see a federal government doctor. Martin walked up to the front desk and stood there for several minutes before being noticed. Without looking up, a harried receptionist shoved an electronic clipboard at him and said, "Fill this out."

Not many seats were available, so he sat down next to a mother and her hyperactive son, who screamed several times and raced back and forth in front of him. He filled out the form as best he could under the circumstances, selecting the "repair" boxes where appropriate, then returned the clipboard to the receptionist, who continued to ignore him.

Fortunately, while he was at the front desk a patient was called and a seat opened up on the other side of the waiting room, far from the screaming child. He sat down next to a nice Indian couple. The woman was very friendly. She had long, black hair and brown eyes, and looked to be about six months pregnant. Her husband was ignoring her by reading an old-fashioned newspaper, and she was just itching to talk to somebody.

"Hello," she said, a white smile brightening her dark features. "Are you getting an implant?"

"No, I'm getting it . . . repaired."

"Repaired? I didn't know you could do that. We're going to get our baby implanted," she said, patting her unborn child and smiling an even bigger smile. "They've got a new procedure where they can go in through the womb."

Martin was shocked. "Why would you want to do that?"

"Why? Because we want our baby to be an American citizen. Sharesh and I were both born in Bangalore. We just became citizens and received our implants. But we want to make sure little Preeti—that's what we're going to call her—enjoys all of the advantages of being an American from the very beginning."

"Oh, I see," Martin said, not really seeing anything at all.

Just then the receptionist called out his name from the front desk. "Mr. . . . Elders?"

"Eldridge," he said.

She was staring at his clipboard. "It says here you were treated for depression last January. Were you on any medication?"

Martin sank down in his chair while everyone in the waiting room waited for his response.

"Yes," he whispered. "I took Serenia for three months."

"Serenia," she repeated much too loudly. Then she wrote something down on the clipboard and, thankfully, left him alone.

The nice Indian lady was sympathetic. "Everybody gets a little depressed now and then."

Martin hung his head and said quietly, "I lost my wife at Christmas."

But their conversation was cut short when the Indian couple was called back to an examination room.

"Wish me luck," she said, smiling that big smile again. Her husband put down the newspaper and escorted her to the back.

Martin picked up the newspaper after they were gone. The headline read, "Trumbull Curbs Freedom of the Press." Unfortunately, half the words in the article were blacked out and he couldn't understand what they were trying to say.

A nurse called his name a few minutes later. "Mr. . . . Elbert?"

"Eldridge," he said.

She was a forty-something blonde with her hair pulled back in a bun. He got up and followed her to a claustrophobic little examination room with a table, guest chair, and brain scanner.

She looked at his clipboard. "It says here you need to get your identity chip repaired."

"Yes, but I need to talk to the doc—"

"Let's check it out."

She set the clipboard down on the examination table and led him over to the brain scanner, which looked like a large glazed doughnut hovering in the air on its side. Positioning his head beneath the doughnut hole, she pressed a button on the device and stood back as the scanner descended over his head and encircled his cranium. Martin knew to stand perfectly still or he'd have to do this all over again.

The nurse read from a display embedded in the wall. "Looks like it's somebody's birthday today. Happy birthday!"

"Thanks."

"And you're a veteran! Which force?"

"I was a radio operator in the navy."

"Don't they have identity clinics at the VA hospital?"

"Not yet."

She touched the screen to navigate to another menu. "Let's check your vitals. Height six-feet-one, weight one-eighty-five. Blood pressure's a little high . . ." She paused to read the screen. "The chip seems to be functioning well, but I'll run a diagnostic."

"I really need to talk to the doc—"

She touched the screen again and Martin was bathed in red light, which made him jump.

"Hold still. It's just part of the procedure." The nurse stared at the display for several minutes before finally saying, "I don't get it. There doesn't seem to be anything wrong with your identity chip. What problems have you been experiencing?"

"Like I said, I just need to speak to the doctor."

She turned to face him. "Well, there's nothing he can do for you if your chip is working, but all right. Have a seat. He'll be here in a few minutes."

Forty-five minutes later the doctor burst into the examination room, obviously in a hurry. He looked to be in his early thirties with disheveled black hair, a rumpled white lab coat, and a pristine silver stethoscope dangling from his neck.

"I'm Dr. Kurtzman," he said briskly. "What seems to be the problem?"

Martin suddenly felt like he was on a time clock, which made him anxious. But he was determined not to be intimidated, so he faced the doctor straight on. "I have a proposition for you," he said.

"A proposition?" Kurtzman grimaced. "Look, Mr.—"

"Eldridge."

"Mr. Eldridge. I have a lot of patients to see today. I don't have time for games."

"This isn't a game," Martin said, getting up to close the door for privacy. "Have a seat." He pointed to the guest chair.

Kurtzman hesitated. "Mr. Eldridge—"

"Please. Humor an old man."

"Oh, all right." Kurtzman grudgingly sat down in the guest chair.

Martin pulled out his change purse and carefully shook his lucky penny into his left palm. Abraham Lincoln's face gleamed in the fluorescent lights of the examination room. Then, placing his right hand on Kurtzman's shoulder, he held the penny before him like it was an offering.

"Do you know what this is?" he asked.

"Of course. It's a penny. An illegal penny, at that."

"Not just any penny. This is a *copper* penny."

Kurtzman wasn't getting it. "And . . .?"

"There are only forty of these pennies in existence. They were minted with copper by accident in 1943. Do you know who this is on the face?"

Kurtzman shook his head. "Should I?"

"It's Abraham Lincoln, sixteenth president of the United States. He freed the slaves." Martin placed the penny in Kurtzman's hand. "This penny is extremely valuable. I've heard of them selling on the black market for over one hundred thousand dollars."

Kurtzman's eyes widened. "One hundred thousand dollars?! For a penny? You've got to be kidding!" He examined the coin more closely.

"Take it, it's yours."

Kurtzman looked up in disbelief. "What?"

"I said take it."

"But . . . but . . . why?"

Martin took a deep breath. "Because, in exchange, you're going to extract the identity chip from my brain."

Kurtzman jumped up from the guest chair. "*That's* your proposition?"

"Yes, that's my proposition."

Kurtzman paced nervously for a few seconds before speaking. "Mr. Eldridge, what you're suggesting is a felony. They could have my license—or worse." He turned the coin over and over in his palm. "Besides, how do I know it's not a fake?"

"Do you have a normal coin?"

Kurtzman reached into his pocket and pulled out several coins, all of them sporting Trumbull's stern profile. Martin withdrew the magnet from his pocket and held it against a Trumbull penny. It stuck. Then he held it against the Lincoln penny and it didn't stick.

"It's made of pure copper," he said. "If it had even the slightest bit of lead in it, it would stick against the magnet."

Martin could see the wheels turning behind Kurtzman's eyes.

"It's a fair exchange," he said. "You get the penny, and I get the chip out of my head. What do you say?"

After a moment, Kurtzman replied, "You understand, of course, that you're effectively renouncing your American citizenship. No more Medicare, no more benefits of any kind."

"That's my problem," Martin said.

Kurtzman paced some more. "And no one will ever know I performed the procedure?"

"No one will ever know."

"I mean, we've never met, right?"

"We've never met."

Kurtzman stuck the penny in his lab coat pocket. "All right, Mr. Eldridge, you've got yourself a deal."

Forty-five minutes later Martin was lying faceup strapped to an operating table in a clean white room, his head held firmly in place by a metal vise. Above him was a bright light, and to the side was what looked like a large silver gun on wheels. Several computer screens were positioned strategically around the room.

Kurtzman entered in his green scrubs and mask. After administering a local anesthetic, he wheeled the gun over to the operating table, positioned it against the right side of Martin's head, and pushed gently. Martin felt a suctioning against his temple.

"That's just to hold it in place," Kurtzman said.

Kurtzman flipped several switches on the gun. A computer image of Martin's brain appeared on one of the screens. The identity chip was a tiny blip on the right side of his cerebral cortex. Kurtzman tapped on one computer screen until an enlarged image of the identity chip appeared on another, then he pressed a red button on top of the gun and Martin felt pressure against the side of his head. A sharp probe entered through his temple and pushed deep into his brain.

A few seconds later Kurtzman announced, "Got it."

The probe slid out of Martin's temple, the pressure dissipated, and the suction was removed. Kurtzman pulled back the gun and applied a gauze pad to Martin's temple.

"Now that wasn't so bad, was it?"

"Yes, it was."

"Sorry about that. I couldn't use a general anesthetic without asking a nurse for assistance." He helped Martin sit up on the table.

"So my identity chip is really gone?"

"Gone forever," Kurtzman said.

The smile on Martin's face could've lit up downtown Atlanta for a week. Thanking Kurtzman profusely, he glided past the waiting room, coasted down to the first floor, and burst out of the building into the sunshine.

Ten minutes later he was back on the interstate, but instead of returning home he headed south out of the city on I-75. Now that he was a free man, Martin was determined to implement the second part of his plan: drive straight through to Miami, buy a boat with the cash he'd been saving up, and sail to the Bahamas to live out the rest of his life in a country that Trumbull had no interest in annexing.

He made it as far as Macon, a two-hour drive from Sugarville, before getting pulled over by the federal police.

A tall officer in dark sunglasses approached the car, his features hard to discern in the bright noonday sun. A second officer waited in the passenger seat of the black cruiser with the windows open.

"Step out of the vehicle, please," the tall officer said.

Martin got out, terrified. "Is there a problem?"

"No problem at all. Hands on the car."

The officer pulled a mobile scanner off his belt, waved it over the back of Martin's head, and read from the display. "Look who we have here. Martin Franklin Eldridge."

"But—but—I thought—"

"You thought what? That you could outsmart the government? That's what they *all* think." He called over to his partner, "We've got another subversive."

The second officer stepped out of the cruiser. He was barely in his twenties.

The tall officer announced, "Martin Franklin Eldridge, you are hereby convicted of attempting to bribe a federal government doctor, a felony punishable by death." He turned to his partner and said, "Why don't you take this one?"

"Really?" the young officer said, smiling.

"Sure, you've got to learn some time."

Martin turned to face them. "Wait a second. Aren't you going to take me in?"

"What for?" the tall officer said.

"What . . . what about a trial?"

The two officers laughed, then the young officer put his gun up to Martin's temple and shot him point-blank.

Martin slumped back against the car and sank to the ground, blood gushing from his head down the side of his face and onto his clothes. As he died, Martin gazed at the tall officer silhouetted against the copper sun and mistook his face for the dignified profile of Abraham Lincoln.

The Last Book

T he old man was on his deathbed when his daughter brought his grandson into the hospital to see him for the last time.

"Take off your headset," the woman told the boy as they entered the cramped private room.

"*Mom*," he whined. The disheveled ten-year-old was on the verge of reaching the next level in his zombie virtual-reality game.

"Now!"

The boy reluctantly removed his headset and looked down at his grandfather. The ashen old man was connected to an intricate series of life-prolonging tubes and looked like he had melted into the bed. His eyes were closed.

"Is he dead yet?"

"Robert!" she scolded, shaking the boy by the arm. She then leaned over the bed. "Dad?"

The old man opened his eyes and smiled faintly in a drug-induced haze. "Barbara," he whispered through paper-thin lips.

"I brought Robert here to see you," she said, pushing the boy forward. She was following through on a promise she'd made to her father to make sure nothing stood between her and her prodigious inheritance.

"Hi, Grandpa," Robert said, edging back from the metal railing as if he were going to catch something.

"Robert," his grandfather said. "Closer."

Robert looked up at his mother.

"Go ahead, honey. It's okay."

Robert leaned over the bed and the old man whispered in his ear. "I have something for you." His grandfather raised a withered hand and pointed to the nightstand.

Barbara picked up a tattered old hardcover book. "This?" she asked. The old man nodded, and she handed the book to Robert.

"What is it?" Robert said, flipping through the musty old pages.

"Why, it's a book, honey," Barbara said. "Don't you remember? We saw a picture of one on TV."

"Oh," he said, clearly not remembering.

"It's . . . it's the last remaining book," the old man said, gathering all the strength he could muster. "I want you to have it. It contains all you need to know to lead a meaningful life."

"Thanks," Robert said, faking a smile as he handed the book back to his mom.

Just then a matronly nurse entered the room clattering a rickety piece of equipment on wheels. "Time for your bloodwork," she sang out to no one in particular.

"Well, we better go now," Barbara said, looking for any excuse to leave. "It's been so good to see you again, Dad. And I brought Robert this time, just like you asked." She turned to her son. "Come on, honey, we don't want to get in the way of the nice nurse."

The old man tried to raise himself up to say goodbye, but by the time he did they were already gone.

Out in the hallway Robert adjusted the settings on his headset.

"Do you want this?" his mother asked, holding the dirty old book at arm's length.

"Mom," Robert said, "you know I can't read."

She dumped the book into a nearby wastebin.

Robert put his headset back on and started playing his game again. The living dead were attacking him from all sides.

The Content Provider

B illy Lockwood was fighting a boss battle in a role-playing game in the finished basement of his parents' Sugarville home when his mother stomped down the stairs and broke his concentration.

"I think I found a job for you," she said, waving her tablet computer in the air like a flag.

He hit pause on the game controller and exhaled. "Another one?"

Billy had been living in his parents' basement ever since graduating from college a year earlier. So far he had no serious prospects for a job other than an entry-level position in the fast-food industry, a position he certainly wasn't going to take as an educated adult with a newly minted BA in English. His parents, now empty nesters, had converted his old bedroom into a home gym as soon as he left for college and seemed surprised their only child was gracing them with his presence once again. His mother had been actively "finding him a job" almost every day for the past six months, but he had to humor her because she was his meal ticket until he found a position that wasn't beneath his dignity.

"Hear me out," she said, sitting down next to him on the unmade sofa bed. She pointed to the screen and read aloud: "Content Provider—write mystery novels for publication on various e-book platforms for Sugarville Books. Previous publications and a bachelors degree in English or journalism required. This is a salaried position with good benefits."

He set the controller down on the bed, grabbed the tablet from her, and studied the job description. "This sounds like a scam," he said. "If they were a legitimate publisher, they'd be located in New York City, not Sugarville, Georgia."

"Well, you yourself said the publishing industry is changing. Maybe this is part of the change. And don't forget you're already a published author with that short story you placed in that mystery magazine. In fact, you're the ideal candidate!"

"Oh, that was just some genre crap. I published *three* short stories in the university's literary journal." He handed the tablet back to her.

"Yeah, but that's not what they're paying for," she said, pointing to the screen. "Anyway, there's only one way to find out. Send them your résumé." She picked up the controller and weighed it in her hand. "That is, of course, unless you're *too busy*."

"Careful," he said, yanking the controller away from her, worried she would push the wrong button and ruin his game. "All right, I'll apply. Can I get back to my game now?"

"Résumé first, game later," she said, standing up.

"Jeez, Mom."

He waited until she left to unpause the game, but with his concentration broken he quickly lost the boss battle. Dispirited, he turned off the console, tweaked his résumé on his laptop to include his publication credits, and sent it off to Sugarville Books.

***

A week later Billy woke up earlier than usual and drove to the outskirts of town for a job interview at Sugarville Books, all to please his mother. The corporate offices were located in a three-story brick building in the middle of Technology Park, and the receptionist directed him to Sam Sanderval's office on the top floor.

"Loved your résumé," Sanderval said, shaking Billy's hand vigorously and showing him to a guest chair. He was an energetic, middle-aged man with black-dyed hair who wore a blue sport coat without a tie. "Can I call you Bill, or Billy?"

"William," he said, trying to distance himself from Sanderval's exuberance.

"William it is. You have some excellent experience, William."

"Thanks, but I haven't even held a real job yet."

"That's true, but you made the best of your college years—excellent grades, working on the literary journal. But I'm particularly impressed with your mystery magazine credit."

"Oh, that was nothing—"

"Now now now, don't discount your accomplishments, William. There are a plenty of guys my age who would kill for a professional credit like that. How much did you make?"

"Three hundred fifty dollars."

"Not bad, but now you can see why you need a full-time job. Writing short stories won't feed the baby."

"I don't have a baby."

"You just wait. First comes the job, then the girlfriend, and—bang! You have to feed the baby! It's the circle of life."

"I see myself as more of a literary writer," Billy said.

"Of course you do. And that's an admirable trait in an idealistic young man. But what are you going to do for money in the meantime? It seems to me you have three options: go on to grad school, flip burgers at a fast-food joint, or come work for me. If you go to grad school you'll end up teaching more than writing, I guarantee it, and I've flipped burgers before—it's greasy. So why don't you come work for me and get paid forty thousand a year to write?"

"Forty thousand a year?!"

"To start."

"Well, maybe . . ."

"That's the spirit! And I already know what your first project will be."

"You do?"

"Remember that detective novel you drafted last November for National Novel Writing Month?" Sanderval asked.

"*Dead on Arrival*? How did you know about that?"

"You posted it on an online workshop."

"Oh, yeah," Billy said. "I forgot. It was really rushed."

"Well, I read it, I like it, and I want you to finish it for me."

"That crap?"

"There you go underestimating yourself again. It's really not that bad, William. Besides, I'll give you three months to polish it up. We only write novels here, no short stories, and you'll get three months to complete each assignment."

"Three months to write an entire novel?!" Billy was incredulous.

"We work fast around here. That's part of our business model. Anyway, you'll have a jump start on this one, and depending on sales, I might ask you to write a sequel or two . . . or three. How does that sound?"

"Um . . . well . . ."

"I'm talking about guaranteed publication of your first novel and forty thousand a year." Sanderval stood up and held out his hand, and Billy felt compelled to do likewise. "So, Monday at eight?"

"I guess so," he said, feeling bullied to accept the job.

Sanderval grabbed Billy's outstretched hand and shook it. "Great to have you on board, William."

Back at the car, Billy had no idea what had just happened, but he knew that landing this job would finally get his mother off his back, and that forty thousand a year would eventually allow him to move out of his parents' basement.

***

On Monday morning Billy was greeted at the reception desk by his new project leader, Alison Cuthbert. Alison was a looker in her late twenties with long blonde hair, emerald eyes, and ample cleavage from which he was unsuccessfully attempting to avert his eyes. His first impression was that here was a woman with whom he could see himself feeding the baby, but his second impression was that he should keep his libido in check when interacting with someone who could influence his performance review.

Alison escorted him to human resources, where he signed intellectual property, nondisclosure, and noncompete agreements and received his building access card.

Then she took him downstairs to the basement to the cubicle farm for novelists.

"I didn't realize this building had a basement," Billy said.

"Oh, yes. We novelists are low man on the totem pole. The screenwriters get the bigger cubes on the second floor."

"What's your genre?" he asked.

"Paranormal romance. It's really hot right now." She smiled broadly and a little too long, making him feel uncomfortable.

She led him through the dimly lit cubicle farm like Virgil guiding Dante through the underworld. He felt like he was lost in a maze in one of his role-playing games, half expecting a balrog to emerge from the labyrinth. The cubicles were filled with expressionless young men and women furiously typing away, most of them with their daily minimum word count pasted to their overhead bins. She showed him where the bathrooms and break rooms were, but hell if he'd be able to find them again on his own. Finally, they reached his cubicle, a six-by-six-foot square beneath a set of foreboding pipes that made constant pinging noises. She switched on the fluorescent light above his desk, but its intermittent flickering was unable to pierce the darkness.

"Home sweet home," she said, smiling. "This is Frank Goodman's old desk. I sure do miss him."

"What happened to him?"

"Um . . . well . . ."

"Tell me."

"He died of overwork. They said it was a stroke, but we all knew better. In fact, right there on that desk. I didn't actually see him, but my understanding is that he laid his head down on the desk one day and everybody thought he was asleep. But it turned out he was dead, and nobody noticed until . . ."

"Until what?" Billy couldn't believe what he was hearing.

"Until he started to smell a few days later. I was his project leader, but he was a great worker who didn't need much supervision. A real self-starter. He didn't have any family, or any friends for that matter. A few of us went to his funeral to pay our respects, but we ended up being the only people there other than a long-lost cousin and the minister."

"Oh my God," Billy whispered, wondering what it would be like to live a life where no one cared if you lived or died. He instinctively backed away from the desk.

"It's been disinfected," she said.

***

At ten o'clock Alison escorted Billy to the first-floor training room for Sanderval's all-hands meeting. Sanderval stood at the front of the theater-style room next to the built-in projector screen, flanked on both sides by flipcharts that read "QBQ = Quantity Before Quality" and "BIC = Butt In Chair." Alison insisted they sit by themselves on the very last row so they could avoid "being called on," and when the lights dimmed, Billy felt like the two of them were out on a date to see a movie.

Sanderval reviewed the second-quarter numbers, which were disappointing, but Billy had trouble paying attention when Alison casually unbuttoned the top two buttons of her red blouse and smiled when she caught him looking. Her bountiful breasts were encased in a lacy, white, see-through bra, and he found himself playing hide-and-seek with her nipples against his better judgment. Billy didn't know much about business, but he was pretty confident that fucking his project leader was not a sound strategy for long-term employment. However, as much as he tried to look away, her breasts called to him like Sirens beckoning Odysseus to his doom, and he found himself utterly mesmerized by their beauty.

As Sanderval discussed the company's plans for the third quarter, Alison removed her black pumps and started massaging her right calf through the nude-colored stocking, looking up to make sure Billy was watching. She wore a short, black skirt that revealed her smooth and sensuous legs, and the methodical motion of her hands on her calf, clearly meant for his enjoyment, was driving him to distraction. When she mercifully leaned back in her chair again, he felt her stockinged foot "accidentally" brush against his leg, and before long she maneuvered it up under his left pant leg and stroked his shin with her soft and warm toes. He tried to stop her a couple of times—after all, they were in public—but she was persistent and he was aroused, and so he lowered his defenses and let her have her way with him.

When the meeting was over and the lights went up, Alison rebuttoned her blouse and put her pumps back on, then leaned over to Billy and whispered, "Would you like to have lunch at my apartment?"

Rendered speechless, Billy nodded yes, stood up, and pulled out his shirttail to hide his erection.

***

Six months later Billy was slaving away in the dead man's cubicle when Sanderval called him upstairs to his office for a meeting on short notice. Billy tucked in his shirt and combed his hair in the blurred reflection of the elevator door, but there was no way to hide his three-day beard growth or the bags under his eyes.

Sanderval was as chipper as usual and seemed to be sporting a new tan. They shook hands and Billy sat down in the same guest chair he had occupied during his job interview, the only other time he had ever been to Sanderval's office.

"I've got some great news, William. *Stiff in the Morgue* is doing even better than *Dead on Arrival*."

"That's terrific, sir."

"It's number one or two in the mystery category of all the major e-book platforms, and it's increasing the sales of the first book, just as we planned. Rick Davenport is starting to become a household name, even if he is just your pseudonym. Have you started the third book in the series yet?"

"Yes, sir. It's called *Autopsy Turvy*. The detective investigates the murder of—"

"Well, that's your business," Sanderval interrupted. "My business is selling books, and I've decided to hire an actor to play the part of your pseudonym on a national book tour."

"You . . . what?"

"We've been getting all sorts of requests for author appearances, and we figure this is the best way to further the brand. We're hiring the same guy who recorded the audiobooks. He's an actor in real life. Not only does he have a great reading voice, but he's incredibly handsome and knows how to control a room. A book tour with this guy out front should increase sales exponentially."

"Oh, I see." Billy paused. "Um, sir, shouldn't Alison be a part of this discussion? After all, she's my project leader."

"There's no need to involve her. The decision's already been made. Anyway, Alison doesn't understand the world of business like us men. In fact, if you play your cards right, you might just end up getting Alison's job one day." Sanderval pushed a form across the desk and handed Billy a pen. "I'll need your John Hancock before we can proceed with the plan. It's just a formality."

Billy felt he had no choice but to do as he was asked. He signed the form without looking at it and pushed it back to Sanderval.

"That's the spirit! By the way, I assigned a screenwriter on the second floor to write a script for the first novel. We might even produce the movie ourselves, depending on how much it costs. Of course, we'd let you visit the set from time to time."

"That's great. I could help with the screenplay if you like."

"Oh, no no no. You just keep on doing what you're doing, William. You're one of the best novelists I've ever hired."

"Thank you, sir."

Sanderval stood up and handed Billy a small white box. "I want to give you this as a token of my appreciation. I realize how much overtime you've been putting in on behalf of the company, and I want to thank you personally for your efforts."

They shook hands again and Sanderval closed his office door.

Billy returned to the dead man's cubicle and opened the box to find a ceramic coffee mug imprinted with the Sugarville Books logo.

***

Billy knocked on the door of Alison's apartment promptly at noon for yet another of their "business lunches." They had been dining on one another at least three times a week since they first met. Alison insisted that meeting clandestinely was good for their relationship because it kept the fantasy element alive, something she probably read (or wrote) in a romance novel once. In fact, there was precious little else *to* their relationship. They never actually ate lunch together, and Billy had taken to picking up fast food on the way back to work after their lovemaking sessions only to eat it alone at his desk.

"Something really strange just happened to me," he said when she opened the door in a see-through black negligee.

"Shhh," she said, placing her index finger over his lips. She took him by the hand, led him into the bedroom, undressed him in a full-length mirror, and laid him down on his back on the king-size bed. Then she got on top of him, pulled back her panties and—ready or not—plugged his joystick into her gaming console. He lost count of her orgasms after three.

When she was done, she rolled off of him and asked, "Did you come?"

"Uh-huh," he lied. He was starting to feel like a human dildo.

"So tell me," she said, lying back on a pillow.

Billy described his surprise meeting with Sanderval, the company's plan to hire an actor to play Rick Davenport, and the gift he was given.

"A coffee mug? What an insult! Marketing has hundreds of them sitting in a cabinet. Look how much money you're making for him, and all he gives you is a coffee mug?!"

He told her about the form Sanderval made him sign and she nearly went ballistic.

"I didn't have a choice," he said.

"You *always* have a choice. And you didn't even read the damned thing. I sure wish I had been there to protect you. Maybe that's why I wasn't invited. When are you going to take control of your career, Billy?"

"It's not a career, Alison, it's a job. I never wanted to be a hack. I want to have a real career as a literary writer, and all I do is write crap all day long."

"Of course it's crap," she said. "That's all anybody reads anymore. We're just giving them what they want. Hell, we're lucky they still read books at all! A novel is just a blueprint for a screenplay anyway. But here's the thing, Billy: what if this really *is* your life? What are you going to do to take control of it? Nobody's going to hand you anything. You're acting like a spectator in your own life. Man up, Billy!" She removed her negligee. "Ready to go again?"

"Um . . . I guess so."

"What's the matter?"

"I'm just a little tired, that's all."

"You're twenty-four frickin' years old! How could you possibly be tired?" She paused. "You don't think I'm a nymphomaniac, do you?"

"Um . . . uh . . . no, of course not. Why would you say that?"

"Lisa thinks I might be a nymphomaniac."

"Who's Lisa?"

"My therapist. She's a really hot redhead. I could ask her to join us for a threesome if you want."

"No, thanks. I think I have my hands full with you."

She smiled and got on top of him again.

**

A few weeks later, Marketing sent out a broadcast email about the new Rick Davenport website they had created, and Billy noticed that "Rick" was scheduled to appear at Barnes & Noble at the Mall of Georgia for a reading the following Saturday. Figuring "Rick" wouldn't recognize him even if he knew who he was, Billy decided to attend the reading to see what the fuss was all about. After all, whether they knew it or not, all those people were really coming to see *him*.

On Saturday morning, a podium and a hundred chairs had been set up in the cloistered upstairs mystery section of the bookstore, and most of the seats were already full. Billy sat on the back row and tried to remain inconspicuous.

The audience clapped enthusiastically when "Rick" was introduced. He was a tall man in his midthirties with dark hair, a ruddy complexion, and movie-star good looks. He appeared supremely confident in spite of the fact that he was impersonating a pseudonym.

"Rick" proceeded to read three short chapters from *Stiff in the Morgue*. Billy was impressed with the tone of voice he established for the wisecracking sympathetic first-person narrator, especially the emphasis he brought to the exaggerated similes. "Rick" also had a talent for changing voices for every character the detective met, which made the story really come alive. Even his female voices were right on target.

But what really impressed Billy was the audience's reaction. They laughed in all the right places, they sat on the edge of their seats during the knife fight, and one woman even started to cry when the detective couldn't save the life of his girlfriend. "Rick" received a standing ovation when he was done, and Billy considered for the first time that maybe the novels he was writing for Sugarville Books weren't such crap after all.

Afterward, Billy decided to go gift shopping for Alison. Her criticism of him being a spectator in his own life had hit him pretty hard, and he thought making a gesture of commitment to her might help him go from being a spectator to being an active participant. He wandered from store to store until a little old lady behind a jewelry counter persuaded him to buy a diamond-studded infinity necklace, an expensive item that she gift-wrapped for him on the spot.

As he was walking down the mall, Billy spotted "Rick" drinking coffee by himself at a table outside of Starbucks. He debated whether or not to introduce himself—wondering fleetingly if a matter/antimatter explosion might ensue from a writer and his pseudonym occupying the same space—but decided it wouldn't do any harm to tell the actor how much he enjoyed his performance.

"Excuse me, aren't you Rick Davenport?"

"Rick" seemed surprised to be recognized. "Why, yes, I am."

"I'm William Lockwood. Does that ring any bells?"

"Um . . . no, I can't say that it does."

Billy lowered his voice to a whisper. "I'm the guy who wrote *Dead on Arrival* and *Stiff in the Morgue*."

"Rick" looked shocked and quickly glanced around to see if they were being watched.

"Don't worry, I'm not going to tell anybody. I just wanted to let you know how much I enjoyed your reading."

"You were there?"

"Yes, in the back."

They shook hands without an explosion ensuing, and "Rick" invited Billy to sit down. After getting acquainted, the actor confided in Billy about the difficulties of being Rick Davenport.

"I'm not complaining, mind you, but I've been away from home for over a month, and most of that time I have to pretend I'm somebody else. It's lonely and exhausting. I'm making good money and the audiences have been great, but I'm not sure how long I can keep up this grueling schedule."

"How much longer do you have?"

"Two more months."

Billy couldn't decide which was worse: writing fourteen hours a day in a basement or performing twenty-four hours a day on the road.

When they ran out of things to say, "Rick" asked, "Can I get a selfie with you?"

"I'm not sure that's such a good idea," Billy said.

"I won't share it with anyone—I mean, other than my husband. I just want to show him those books were written by a real live human being. He thinks they were written by a computer."

"Okay," Billy said, and he leaned in so "Rick" could capture their picture on his smartphone.

**

On Monday morning at nine o'clock, Sanderval showed up at Billy's cubicle with the company's uniformed security guard in tow. "Sorry, William, but I'm afraid I have to terminate your employment. Please collect up your belongings and follow me out of the building."

"Wh—wh—*what?*" Billy said.

Sanderval held up a printout of the selfie "Rick" had taken of the two of them.

"Where did you get that?" Billy said, the blood draining from his face.

"This is an unauthorized photograph taken on a company-sponsored smartphone," Sanderval said, crushing the paper into a ball and tossing it into the wastebasket.

"So you've been *spying* on Rick Davenport?"

"That's a harsh word. I prefer the word *monitoring*. You know as well as I do that Rick Davenport doesn't exist, but it's imperative that the reading public never find that out, and I'll do everything in my power to ensure the integrity of the brand."

"But I didn't take that photograph, Rick did. Why don't you fire *him?*"

"Oh, he's been disciplined, to be sure, but he's already established as the face of Rick Davenport, and he's become an indispensable part of our business strategy going forward. I'll grant you he's not the sharpest tool in the shed, but you, on the other hand, should have known better."

"What about *Autopsy Turvy?*"

"Oh, I'll just give that to Alison to finish. Hell, I could finish it myself if I had the time. Like I've said a thousand times before, nobody cares about quality. Readers *expect* the books in a series to get worse as they go along, and yet they continue to buy them. I don't know why—it's a mystery. So your services are no longer required, William. It's as simple as that. Just remember you're still obligated to keep our little secret, and if you ever tell anyone you wrote those books, I'll sue your pants off and have you thrown in jail. That's a promise, not a threat."

Stunned, Billy collected up his belongings, handed his badge to Sanderval, and followed Sanderval and the security guard out of the building, never to return.

***

Knowing Alison had taken the day off, Billy drove to her apartment instead of heading home to face his mother's wrath. He had planned to give her the infinity necklace that evening at dinner and had the gift box hidden in his pocket when he knocked on her door.

"Who is it?" she said through the closed door.

"It's me, Billy."

She cracked the door open but kept the chain engaged. "Billy, what are you doing here?"

"Sanderval fired me. Can I come in?"

"You should've called first. I'm busy."

"Busy? What do you mean you're busy?"

She whispered, "Lisa is here with me."

"Lisa? I thought she was your *therapist*."

"Not anymore. It would be unethical for her to be my therapist and . . . and . . . my lover."

"Your *lover*?" he said, his stomach dropping through the floor.

"You should've called first." She closed the door.

Billy stared at the door for a few minutes in disbelief, then walked back downstairs, threw the infinity necklace into a green dumpster, and drove back to his parents' house.

***

Three weeks later Billy was back in his parents' basement, awake at 3:00 a.m. because of a stifling depression that had descended on him like a black cloud. He tried to play his favorite role-playing game but couldn't muster the enthusiasm he once felt for it. He opened up his laptop and surfed the web, but the first thing he saw was an advertisement for *Autopsy Turvy* with a picture of Rick Davenport's smiling face next to the cover.

Sitting blank-faced on the unmade bed, Billy's gaze settled on an exposed ceiling beam in the unfinished storage area of the basement.

It would be so easy to make an improvised rope with his bedsheets.

It would be so easy to loop that rope around the exposed beam and create a noose.

It would be so easy to hang himself from the noose and put an end to his suffering.

But that's not what he did.

Instead, he opened the word processor on his laptop and started to write a short story. It was about a young man who fails at business and fails at love but gets up on his feet and starts his life over again. He wasn't sure what the moral of the story would be, but he was hoping that one would come to him by the time he reached the end.

Masks

T heir custom-tailored costumes arrived from Dangerous Pretensions just in time for the Halloween party. Mark and Amelia Richmond donned their masks and outfits, slid into the silver Mercedes, and glided down the interstate from Sugarville to Buckhead.

"You look terrific," Mark said, staring at Amelia's voluptuous body trapped inside a green-plaid schoolgirl's uniform. Her hand-painted mask was spotted with freckles, and her long brown hair was pulled back in a ponytail.

She smiled. "I thought you might like this." They'd agreed to keep their costumes a secret until the day of the party. "You don't look half bad yourself." Mark wore a pirate's outfit and a mask sporting a patch over one eye and a scar down the cheek.

They were in their early thirties and had been married for ten years, but they felt like they hardly knew each other anymore because they were always working. Mark was a high-powered investment banker who was constantly traveling, and Amelia was an in-demand CPA who often put in eighty hours a week. It was Amelia's idea to spice up their sex life with role-playing, and Mark had suggested they use his company's annual Halloween party as an excuse to go through with it.

They reached the Ritz-Carlton fashionably late. After the grand entrance, the cold martinis, the hot canapes, and the obligatory chitchat, they found themselves slow dancing in the middle of the ballroom with all eyes on them.

"Not so close," Amelia protested. This was the most aroused she'd seen her husband in quite some time.

"Would you like to come up to my room, little girl?"

"What about our friends?"

"Those posers? They'll have to find their own dates."

"Well, if you insist."

They slipped out of the party and booked a room for the evening. Closing the door, Mark slowly undressed Amelia, savoring every moment as he released her lovely breasts from the tight uniform. Soon they were both naked.

"What about the masks?" she asked.

"Let's leave them on," he whispered, French-kissing her through the mouth holes.

Mark imagined himself as a real pirate introducing a virgin to the ways of the world, and Amelia imagined herself as an innocent being ravished by Blackbeard. Abandoning themselves to their roles like method actors losing themselves in their parts, they not only had the best sex of their marriage but of their lives. Afterward, drunk and exhausted, they fell asleep, forgetting to remove the masks.

When they awoke in the morning they turned to face each other and laughed, but after several desperate moments of trying to help each other pull them off, they discovered that the masks were permanently affixed to their faces.

The Theory of Doors

C hief among Henry Klein's phobias was the fear of dying alone. That's why he persuaded his wife, Rachel, to agree to a suicide pact to commemorate their fiftieth wedding anniversary. He imagined them swallowing cyanide pills together, lying down on their king-size bed, and cradling each other in one final embrace. Unfortunately, Rachel died unexpectedly in a car crash two years before the appointed date, leaving Henry grief-stricken and terrified that his worst nightmare would come true. He considered killing himself right after the funeral—even to the point of holding a loaded revolver to his temple one dark night—but he simply lacked the courage to go through with it on his own. There was something romantic in a loving couple choosing to end their lives together that was missing from a run-of-the-mill suicide. After much deliberation, Henry decided he would just have to find another woman with whom he could share a meaningful death.

Working through an online dating agency for mature adults, Henry arranged a lunch date with a lady named Constance Reynolds at Sugarville's most popular Mexican restaurant. He arrived a half hour early and sat at a booth with a strategic view of the entrance, anxiously sipping sweet tea and forcing himself to breathe deeply. He stood to greet Constance when she arrived, escorted her to their table, and helped her duck under a brightly colored donkey-shaped piñata to reach her seat. She had to be over sixty to join the agency, but with her light-auburn hair, trim figure, and modest-but-appealing black jumpsuit, she didn't look a day over fifty. Of course, the fact that she was attractive made Henry all the more nervous, and he found himself talking nonstop in between forkfuls of his chimichanga.

"I think of life as a series of doors," he said. "When you're young, you're presented with an almost infinite number of doors from which to choose, and the future seems limitless. But as you mature and you've chosen and walked through a number of doors already, there are fewer and fewer doors to select from, and once you select a particular door, it closes behind you and locks forever. Finally, in old age, you're presented with only two doors, and you know for a fact that once you've made your choice, you must walk down that long, final corridor alone. You'll never know if you made the right decision because you can never find out what was behind the other door."

Constance, barely picking at her chalupa, smiled and nodded in all the right places, emboldening Henry to proceed.

"But then I had another thought. After all these years of choosing doors and having them lock behind me, what if I decided to stop choosing? There's no law against it, you know. In fact, not choosing is a choice in and of itself, a choice that's not forced on you, the only choice you can really make on your own."

"But how can you stop choosing?" she asked.

Henry took a deep breath. "By ending your life before your life is ended for you. I'm sitting here on the threshold of those two doors, doors that look exactly the same to me, and I really don't want to know what's on the other side of either one of them. Why not just stop right here before I have to make that choice?

Her smile faded and she whispered, "You mean . . . *suicide*?"

"Yes, but not alone. That's the beauty of my plan. I'm looking for someone to share that final journey with me—the journey into the unknown."

"*What?*" Constance threw her napkin down on the plate and stood up. "Well, it's not going to be me. I came here for a casual lunch, not a murder-suicide pact."

Henry jumped up and bumped his head on the donkey piñata, causing it to swing back and forth like a pendulum. "But—but—we'd get to know each other first."

She turned to face him. "You don't need a girlfriend. You need a therapist. Thanks for lunch."

Constance fled the restaurant like a bandito escaping the federales.

Henry reached up to stabilize the donkey piñata, but despite his best efforts it detached from the ceiling, crashed to the floor, and broke open, covering him with multicolored confetti.

***

The next candidate, Nancy Unruh, met Henry at a nearby Chinese restaurant for an early dinner. They sat under a large, three-dimensional relief of the Great Wall of China. Nancy was a high school English teacher in her early sixties with dirty blonde hair pulled back severely from her face and half-frame reading glasses that she forgot to take off when she wasn't reading. After a dinner of sesame chicken and shrimp with lobster sauce, Henry started in on his theory of doors and the need to find a suicide companion.

"If I were you," Nancy said, "I'd be concerned about my immortal soul. Suicide is a mortal sin in some circles."

"I'm not Catholic," he said.

"Neither am I, I'm a recovering Southern Baptist. But there are good reasons why Catholics think that way. People only commit suicide out of desperation, when they lose all hope. The sin isn't necessarily in the act of committing suicide, but in willfully giving up on hope. That's why suicides are considered lost souls."

"I haven't given up on hope," Henry said. "I just realize that the best years of my life are probably behind me, and I want to end it on my own terms while I still have my wits about me."

Nancy looked over the top of her glasses. "That's God's job, not yours."

"And what if I don't believe in God?"

"Even so," she said, "how do *you* know the best years of your life are behind you? Do you have a crystal ball?"

"Well, no . . ."

"Look, Henry, how old are you?"

"Seventy-three," he said.

"And do you have any major illnesses?"

"Not that I know of."

"What about money? Do you have enough to live on comfortably?"

"Well, yes," he said. "I have a pension from the university."

"So you feasibly have twenty or so years left to enjoy. You could travel, take up a hobby—fall in love, for heaven's sake."

"Or I could watch my body deteriorate and spend the rest of my life eating cat food."

There was a long pause during which Henry looked up at the Great Wall of China, which seemed to descend from the mural and divide the dinner table in half.

Finally, Nancy said, "Well, I guess we'll just have to agree to disagree. Frankly, I doubt you'll find a woman who will go along with your plan. Most people go out on dates to find partners for *life*, not death. Maybe if you meet the right person you'll change your mind."

Henry paid for the dinner and they parted amicably.

***

Henry considered canceling his third date because he hadn't slept well thinking about what Nancy had said. What if she was right, not about the God part but about the cowardice of giving up on hope? Anyway, maybe God was just another name for hope, and by turning his back on hope he was turning his back on God—whoever or whatever that might be. He was starting to think that by committing suicide he would be making a mockery of his life up until that point, including the most meaningful part, his time with Rachel. He kept mulling that idea over and over again in his mind and started to have second thoughts about his plan.

And then there was Nancy herself. Of course, no one could ever replace Rachel, but he had enjoyed talking to Nancy, felt comfortable in her presence, and sensed a spark between them. Maybe it had been a bad idea to bring up his philosophy of life so early in the relationship. He hadn't dated in so long he hardly knew what the rules were anymore. He could apologize for that faux pas and see if she'd like to go out on a second date. He decided to call her.

But that would have to wait for now. He had arranged all three dates in advance, and Henry was nothing if not dependable, so he found himself sitting in a dimly lit back booth in his favorite Italian restaurant waiting for Maggie Treadwell to arrive. Unfortunately, Maggie was late. He took a sip of his second glass of chianti and scanned the restaurant for a lost older woman. He was about to give up and head home when a decidedly younger woman with short, black hair and a ring through the side of her nose appeared at his table.

"Are you Henry Klein?" she asked.

"Yes."

She threw her purse on the seat opposite him and sat down. "I'm Maggie." Her dark-red lipstick and pale white skin gave her an otherworldly appearance, and her black lace dress made her look like she was on her way to a funeral.

"You're—?"

"I know, I'm a little young for you. Do you mind?" She grabbed his wine and promptly swallowed half of it. "Wow, that's *good*. I hacked my granny's account."

"You *what*?"

"The dating site for 'mature adults.' Her name is Maggie Treadwell too."

"Why would you do that?"

"Because guys my age bore the hell out of me. They're just a bunch of *posers*. They're too busy following their cocks to have anything intelligent to say. I saw your profile on the site. I liked the quotes you put out there."

"Um . . . thanks." Henry felt partly aghast and partly flattered, torn between the desire to leave and the curiosity of finding out more about this audacious young lady. However, when he glanced down at her ample bosom rising from the tight lace corset, he decided to stay.

"I particularly liked the one that went, 'If God did not exist, it would be necessary to invent him.' What did you mean by that?"

"It's Voltaire. It's just a clever way of him saying that he didn't really believe in God. He argued that man created God in his own image, not the other way around. I used to teach his philosophical writings in one of my classes at the university."

"Oh, so you're a professor?"

"I was. I'm retired now."

He looked down at her cleavage and wondered if a man his age could still get lucky.

"Is that what *you* believe?" she asked.

"More or less. I believe that man created the concept of God as a survival mechanism. The only way humanity has been able to survive up until now was to have a baseline code of ethics that spanned all religions. Evolution itself was amoral. We needed an artificial means to overcome our natural instincts, and we called that God. In a sense, God is a collaborative art form."

"*Intense,*" she said. Henry was happy to have an audience again. This girl could easily have been one of his students.

"But belief in God just isn't enough anymore. That idea worked for centuries, but ever since science backed God into a corner, even the most devout have had trouble believing in Him. I think it's up to us individually to come up with our own meaning, our own God, if you will. You can't expect to do it by joining some kind of group. But that's a monumentally difficult task for most people, maybe even impossible. It certainly takes a good imagination, something that's in short supply these days."

"So how would you go about doing that—making your own meaning?"

"By taking control of your life and accepting total responsibility for your actions. It's not up to any authority—work, family, government, or even religion. And it's scary. It never fails to amaze me how otherwise free Americans are willing to give up their freedom for an illusory sense of belonging and comfort. You have to have the courage to be an outsider."

"Well, that's not a problem for me," she said.

And so Henry launched into his theory of doors once more, but his heart wasn't in it. Perhaps he had taken his philosophy a step too far. Was he trying to play God by taking his fate into his own hands, and was it wrong of him to attempt to convince another person to go along with his plan? However, he managed to finish the analogy as if he still believed it, having spent so many years trying to convince himself of its veracity.

When he was done, Maggie said, "So let me get this straight. By committing suicide you'd be taking control of your life and giving meaning to your death?"

"Yes," he said. "After all, suicide is the fundamental question of philosophy, and how you answer that question helps determine what kind of person you are."

"Uh-huh. It seems to me there's a much simpler explanation."

"What's that?"

"Life really is meaningless, and you're afraid to admit it. You're twisting yourself into a pretzel trying to pretend there's meaning where it doesn't exist. I don't think your suicide would be any more meaningful than anybody else's death. It seems to me you think too much and feel too little. What are you so afraid of?"

At first, Henry was taken aback that this young girl would openly challenge him. But when he looked into her eyes and realized she was being sincere, he took a deep breath, centered himself, and made a conscious effort to identify his feelings. Finally, he said, "I'm afraid of dying alone."

"Now, that wasn't so difficult, was it? I don't know why you didn't just say so in the first place. Nobody wants to die alone."

She reached into her purse, pulled out a small handgun, and laid it on the table.

"What's *that*?" Henry asked, his eyes widening. "Is it *real*?"

"Of course it's real. A girl's got to protect herself."

"What . . . what are you going to do with it?"

"I'm going to determine if you have the courage of your convictions. You see, I don't need to build an elaborate house of cards to tell *me* life is meaningless. I feel it in my gut. I've never believed in God, and if there's no God then there's no basis for ethics either. So it doesn't really matter what we do. There's no point to any of it. The only point is to end your suffering as soon as possible. So if you really want a suicide partner, here I am."

She released the safety and pushed the gun toward him, but he recoiled from it as if it were a snake.

"What are you waiting for? This is your ticket out."

Henry started to shake and pushed back into the seat cushion. Although he had convinced himself of the validity of suicide intellectually, now that he faced an actual emotional choice with irreversible consequences, he was afraid.

"I thought so. After all that talk, you're just a poser like everybody else." She picked up the gun and pointed it at him. "But at least you don't have to die alone."

"God, no!" he shouted.

She shot him three times in the chest point-blank. Pain began seeping into his body as blood started pouring out. As he was losing consciousness, he watched her put the gun to her temple and say, "There's no such thing as a meaningful death." Then she blew her brains out.

Henry slumped over the table, his final door having been chosen for him.

Lifesaver

Project Director Bob Morton had just taken a big bite out of his breakfast bar when Phil Richardson, his star software analyst, rang him up on his office phone.

"Phil!" Bob answered irritably. "Are you stuck in traffic? The project review starts in ten minutes!"

"No, no traffic. I won't be coming in today, Bob."

"What? Are you sick? I'm counting on you for the ERP software presentation."

"No, I'm not sick," Phil said. "I . . . I killed Marjorie and the girls last night."

"So . . . you'll be a few minutes late?"

"More than a few minutes. I stabbed Marjorie sixteen times."

"Well, if I have to I can postpone till this afternoon." Bob sighed. "But I'd hate to go any later than that because the VP of development flew in from the coast just to be here."

"You just don't get it, Bob. I won't be coming in today. I may not be coming in at all, ever again. I called the police. They're on their way over here."

"Jesus, Phil, you're putting me in an awful bind. You're the only one who understands this damned ERP system. Hell, I don't even know what it stands for."

"Enterprise resource planning. Didn't you get my email?"

"What email?"

"The one from last night. I sent it around midnight, right before I drowned Lillian and April in the bathtub."

"Well, I haven't checked my email yet." Returning to his laptop, Bob browsed through his inbox. "Oh, here it is. Project review, right?"

"Right. The PowerPoint's attached. That should give you everything you need for the meeting."

"Wow, Phil, you're a true professional. It won't be the same without you presenting, though."

"I'm sure you'll do fine, Bob. Just remember to gloss over the details, like you always do."

"Thanks, Phil. You're a lifesaver."

Setting the World to Rights

I never wanted to hire a security guard to patrol the subdivision, but when the other members of the homeowners association insisted that our resident peeping tom might escalate into a full-blown home-invading rapist, I was required as president to pursue the matter. Everyone knew the culprit was probably Nate Fillmore, a Sugarville High senior who was always getting into trouble, but no one had been able to catch him in the act. So the board chose to treat the entire neighborhood like an unruly group of high school students being held after class, and they appointed me head of detention.

Finding a security guard was easy enough, but finding one who would work nights for low pay proved more difficult. I finally settled on a local agency that assigned an elderly gentleman named Peter Genworth, a retired English professor who said he needed the money to supplement his social security income. He seemed like an affable enough fellow, and considering his primary duties would consist of driving around the neighborhood to make his presence known and sitting at the pool parking lot waving to residents, I hired him on the spot. He was happy to have the work, and I was happy to check that task off my to-do list and report my success back to the homeowners association.

One night on my way home from the hospital, I saw Peter sitting alone in his car reading a book, and I suddenly felt sorry for him. I've read several medical studies that suggest men who retire early also die early because they lose their purpose in life, and here was a man who had been a tenured professor at Emory University suffering the indignity of working as a security guard just to make ends meet. He looked lonely and bored beneath the dim parking-lot light, so I decided to pay him a visit.

I parked my Porsche at the house and walked to the pool, still wearing my black racing jacket and leather gloves to fend off the sudden April drizzle. Peter's car was a white SUV with a makeshift "Security" decal affixed to the door and a removable amber warning light positioned on top. He was reading a well-thumbed paperback and seemed surprised to see me, but rolled down his window as I approached.

"Is everything all right?" he asked.

"Everything's fine. I just thought you could use a little company."

"Oh, sure. Why don't you come in out of the rain?"

He started to move his holstered revolver from the passenger side seat to the front floorboard, but I stopped him. "That's all right. I'll just sit in the back." I got in behind him and closed the door. "What're you reading?"

"Some whodunit. I just read for fun now that I'm retired and don't have to prove anything to anyone anymore." He raised the driver-side window to keep out the rain, which had turned into a steady downpour and was fogging up the windows.

"Can I take a look?"

"Sure." He handed me the book. It was one of those series mystery novels with the author's name at the top in a bigger font than the title. "It's the thirteenth book in the series, and I've read every last one of them. The detective is going to catch the bad guy again, no doubt."

"If you know the ending, why bother reading it?"

"That's the nature of genre fiction. The ending is never in doubt, especially if the author wants to sell his book to Hollywood. In a mystery novel, the detective always catches the bad guy; in a romance novel, the heroine always marries Mr. Right; and in a science-fiction novel, humanity always comes one step closer to understanding the universe."

"I never thought about it that way," I said, unzipping my racing jacket.

"It's all predicated on false hope—the false hope that order can be restored to society, the false hope that true love can be found, and the false hope that man can understand the universe. People need those beliefs to have the strength to go on living. If we stopped believing in those fictions, we'd all become nihilists and civilization would collapse. Genre fiction is all about setting the world to rights."

"Setting the world to rights. I like that." As I handed the book back to him, the novel "slipped" from my grasp and landed on the console between the seats. When he reached down to pick it up, I pulled the nylon rope out of my jacket, looped it over his head, and pulled it tight. He lost consciousness in ten seconds and died in three minutes.

I stuffed the rope, novel, and revolver inside my racing jacket, zipped it up, and walked back to my house in the rain.

A detective showed up on my doorstep the next day after I returned home from performing a heart-transplant operation. He was trying his best not to look like a cliché, but with his tan raincoat and flip-top notepad, it was obvious he had read his fair share of whodunits.

"Are you Dr. Everett Franklin?" he asked.

"Yes," I said.

"I'm Detective Marshall with the Sugarville Police Department." He flashed his badge. "I understand you're the president of the homeowners association."

"Yes, I am. Would you like to come in?"

"That won't be necessary," he said. "Do you live here alone?"

"Yes. My wife died three years ago."

"I'm sorry to hear that." He looked at his notepad. "Dr. Franklin, were you responsible for hiring a Peter . . . Genworth . . . as a security guard?"

"Yes, I was. Is something wrong?"

"I'm sorry to say that Mr. Genworth is dead," he said.

"Dead? Oh my God! What happened?"

"We're still trying to determine that. When was the last time you saw him?"

"Um . . . I just saw him last night . . . when I got back from the hospital. I guess it was around nine o'clock. He waved to me from his car when I entered the subdivision. Did he have a heart attack or something?"

"No," he said. "Frankly, we believe he was murdered."

"Murdered? Here in the subdivision?"

"Yes."

"Jesus Christ."

"I understand you hired him fairly recently?"

126

"Just last week," I said. "We were having problems with a peeping tom."

"A peeping tom?" He made another note. "Did you inform the police?"

"Well, I didn't personally, but I imagine one of my neighbors did. Anyway, I persuaded the board to hire a security guard as a stopgap measure."

"Why stopgap?" he asked.

"Well, we have several teenage boys who will be going off to college in the fall, and I figure the peeping tom issue will resolve itself, if you know what I mean."

"So you suspect one of them of being the peeping tom?"

"Boys will be boys," I said.

"Anyone in particular?"

"Oh, no no no. I have absolutely no evidence. Just a hunch."

"Dr. Franklin, this is now a murder investigation, and I have to pursue every lead."

"But I don't want to get the boy in trouble," I said.

"He may be in more trouble than you know."

"All right, all right. Nate Fillmore."

He made another note. "And where does this Nate Fillmore live?"

I pointed to the house across the street.

After he left, I watched Detective Marshall through my plantation blinds as he interviewed Nate for a solid fifteen minutes before getting back in his car and driving off.

***

That night I put on my racing jacket and gloves and walked across the street to the Fillmore's house, the revolver and rope hidden under my jacket but the novel held openly in my gloved right hand. Nate answered the door. He was a good-looking young man with short, brown hair and blue eyes who wore an untucked pullover shirt, a pair of jean shorts, and no shoes.

"Hey, Nate," I said.

"Hey, Dr. Franklin."

"Is your dad around?"

"No, he's over in London with Mom and Amy for a couple of weeks."

"Oh, damn, I forgot!" I said. "Could you give this book back to him? I borrowed it a few months ago and I've been meaning to return it." I handed him the novel.

"Sure," he said, placing the book on a small table in the foyer.

"Thanks," I said, pretending to leave but turning back around. "By the way, did your dad ever fix that cooling unit in the basement?"

"I don't think so," he said. "Dad said he was going to hire an HVAC guy."

"HVAC? They don't know the first thing about wine cellars. Let me take a look. Maybe I can fix it before he gets back."

"Okay," he said.

I closed the front door and headed for the interior basement door.

"Can I ask you a question, Dr. Franklin?"

"Sure, Nate."

"Have you heard anything about there being a peeping tom in the neighborhood?"

"A peeping tom?" I said. "No. Why do you ask?"

"Oh, nothing. Just a rumor."

"That's a strange rumor. Why bother being a peeping tom in this day and age when you can find plenty of naked girls on the internet?" He laughed, and I opened the basement door and started to descend. "Back in a second," I said, leaving the door ajar.

When I reached the basement, I walked past the mahogany bar and the home theater to the wine cellar, a soundproof room I had helped Nate's dad build five years earlier. Keeping the lights as dim as possible, I removed the revolver from my racing jacket, unholstered it, released the safety catch, and set it down on the cooling unit. Then I walked back to the bottom of the stairs.

"Hey, Nate. Could you bring me a screwdriver?"

"Flathead or Phillips?"

"Phillips."

I walked back to the wine cellar and hid behind the thick wooden door with the revolver. When Nate appeared in the dim light, I put the revolver up to his temple and pulled the trigger. He died immediately. I placed the revolver in his right hand with his index finger on the trigger, picked up the screwdriver, and selected a bottle of cabernet that wouldn't be missed.

Climbing the basement stairs to the foyer, I picked up the novel with my left gloved hand, ascended to the second floor, and hid the novel and rope under Nate's bed. I took the Phillips head screwdriver into his sister Amy's bedroom and removed the video camera I had hidden in her bathroom six months earlier. Zipping up the camera and wine bottle in my jacket, I walked back downstairs and replaced the screwdriver in the kitchen drawer. I locked the front door with the extra key I had made when the Fillmores weren't looking, and returned to my house unnoticed.

Later that night I treated myself to several glasses of cabernet and a video of Amy undressing.

**

Two days later Detective Marshall showed up on my doorstep again, still wearing the raincoat and holding the notepad.

"Dr. Franklin, we've had a significant development in the case," he said.

"Really?" I said. "That's great!"

"I can't go into detail, but I wanted to let you know that we identified the murderer."

"You did?"

"It was Nate Fillmore."

"Nate Fillmore?" I said. "But why?"

"As best we can determine, Peter Genworth figured out that Nate was the peeping tom, and Nate murdered him to keep him quiet."

"Oh my God!" I said. "Did you take Nate into custody?"

"No, he killed himself before we could arrest him."

"He *what*?"

"We found his body in his parents' basement." He pointed to the house across the street. "It's a real tragedy. I guess I must've spooked him when I talked to him a few days ago. We've already contacted his parents. They're on their way back from London now. Anyway, I just wanted to thank you for your help. I couldn't have broken the case without you."

"His parents are going to be devastated," I said.

"Well, it's one thing to be a peeping tom, but quite another to be a murderer. Just between you and me, he's probably better off this way. He would've spent the rest of his life in jail, and I wouldn't wish that on my worst enemy, let alone a good-looking young man like that, if you know what I mean."

"Well, I'm glad I could help you out," I said. "But this is terrible news. The community is going to be extremely upset about this. I'll have to call a homeowners association meeting right away. Anyway, thank you for telling me first. You've done a terrific job in solving this case. It must be very satisfying for you to be able to set the world to rights."

"I beg your pardon?" he said.

"You know, restore order to society and all that."

"Huh?"

"You caught the bad guy."

"Oh, yeah," he said. "Actually, it's more like he caught himself. I guess he couldn't live with the thought of being a murderer, or at least he couldn't live with the thought of *getting caught* for being a murderer. We'll never know for sure. Either way, this case is closed."

He thanked me again and departed.

Now that the peeping tom issue has been resolved, I should have no difficulty convincing the board to avoid hiring any more security guards. I'm looking forward to consoling the Fillmores when they return from London, especially Amy. I'm starting to think of that girl like the daughter I never had.

The Bag Man and the Bag Lady

T ony Bartone sat down on a park bench facing the amphitheater with a briefcase full of money and a bad case of the jitters. Surely they'd never find him here. The Town Green in Sugarville, Georgia, was the perfect place to hide out from the mob on Christmas Eve. He had grown up here before his family had relocated to New Jersey. Now he was looking for a fresh start, and he needed some time to figure out his next move.

As the sun set and the Christmas tree lights flickered on, Tony noticed a bedraggled old woman pushing a rusted grocery cart down the sidewalk in his direction. Her hair was gray and stringy, her coat tattered and full of holes, and all her worldly possessions appeared to be contained in shopping bags inside the grocery cart. Although she sighed heavily as she sat down on the bench next to him, she seemed to be in good spirits.

"Merry Christmas!" she said.

"Merry Christmas," he replied, but he really just wanted to be left alone. He was trying to decide between the Bahamas and Argentina, wondering where the Cosa Nostra would be least likely to find him.

"Say," the old lady asked, "aren't you Tony Bartone?"

He nearly jumped off the bench and made a run for it. This was the last place on earth he thought he would be recognized.

"I'm Anna. Anna Davenport."

The name sounded familiar, but he couldn't quite place the face.

"Mrs. Davenport, the band director?"

"Oh, *Mrs. Davenport*." Tony had played in the Sugarville High School Marching Band for three years before moving to New Jersey. "I hardly recognized you. What . . . what happened to you?"

"Well, you know, they never did pay teachers much . . . and then there was the divorce . . . and one thing led to another . . ."

"I'm sorry to hear that. You were my favorite teacher in high school."

"Why, thank you, Tony. That means a lot to me. And you were one of my best students. I still remember your trumpet solo on 'Live and Let Die.' You had God-given embouchure."

"That was one of the proudest moments of my life, maybe *the* proudest moment." Tony became quiet thinking about how his life had gone downhill ever since he'd left Sugarville. After a long pause, he said, "Mrs. Davenport, I've done some things I'm not proud of since I left high school. Unforgiveable things, really."

"Nonsense, Tony. Remember what I told you?"

"You mean 'Early is on time and on time is late'?"

"No, not that one. 'To be forgiven, you must learn how to forgive.' And sometimes you have to start by forgiving yourself."

"Oh, yeah, I'd almost forgotten. That makes a lot of sense." He smiled. "Tell me, Mrs. Davenport, how can you remain so positive after all you've been through?"

"Simple, Tony: I've never lost my faith in humanity."

They both sat for a long time, looking at the Christmas tree lights and enjoying each other's silent company. Tony reflected on the life he'd been leading and wondered if he could ever forgive himself. Well, he certainly wouldn't find forgiveness hiding out in some foreign country. Maybe he could put the pieces of his life back together again right here in Sugarville. Finally, he got up and said, "It was so good to see you again." He dropped the briefcase into the shopping cart, said "Merry Christmas, Mrs. Davenport!" and walked off into the night.

It was good to be home.

A Frank Discussion

As the cell door closed behind them, the new inmates sat down opposite one another on flimsy cots in the orange jumpsuits provided to them by the Sugarville Correctional Facility. Both were named Frank, but one was older and the other younger.

"What're you in for?" asked Younger Frank.

"It's not my fault," said Older Frank. He paused. "I . . . I killed my wife."

"How can that not be your fault?"

"It was the gel. Look, I don't want to talk about it."

Younger Frank frowned. "What the hell else are we going to talk about? We're going to be in here for the rest of our frickin' lives—we have to talk about *something*. Besides, you can't just say 'It was the gel' and leave it at that. Now you've piqued my curiosity."

"All right, all right," said Older Frank. "It's just . . . embarrassing. It's *sexual*."

"Even better."

Older Frank took several deep breaths before embarking on his story. "Well, it started about a year ago. I went to the doctor's office for my annual physical, and he diagnosed me with low testosterone."

"Oh, you mean you couldn't get it up?"

"No, no, nothing like that. When a man reaches middle age, his metabolism starts to slow down, and some men can't produce enough testosterone anymore. As a result, they have to add it to their bodies artificially. I was suffering from depression and a lack of desire. The equipment was working just fine, but my desire to use it had diminished, which, as you can imagine, created a problem with my wife."

"That selfish bitch," Younger Frank said.

"Watch it, buddy. That's my wife you're talking about."

"The one you killed?"

"Anyway, my doctor prescribed testosterone gel that I had to rub on my upper arms and shoulders every day. At first, nothing much changed, but after a few weeks my depression lifted and I began to desire Melanie again. We started having sex once a week just like the old days, and each time was better than the last."

"So what was the problem?"

"Well, we enjoyed it so much we both wanted more. Without telling Melanie, I started to apply double doses in the morning. Then we started to have sex two or three times a week, like when we first met. We felt like horny teenagers. So I started applying triple doses and looking for new sources of the gel because I kept running out. At first I went to different doctors for multiple prescriptions, but then I found this one doctor who was willing to prescribe liquid testosterone that I could shoot directly into my veins."

"Jesus, a testosterone junky," said Younger Frank.

"I couldn't stop. Our sex life was going great, and our marriage was improving, but—"

"But what?"

"But then I started to see physical changes in my body. My teeth and nails grew faster and sharper, and my hair became thicker and darker, and pretty soon my entire body was covered in brown fur."

"Whoa! What did your wife think?"

"Oh, Melanie loved every minute of it, up to a point. But I had to shave three times a day and wear long-sleeve shirts just to go out in public. It was like I was leading a double life—mild-mannered accountant during the day, and sex-crazed maniac at night. And it was every night, night after night, sometimes the whole night through. Melanie started calling me her 'caveman.' But the more I devolved the more she seemed to like it, so I kept on injecting myself, until . . . until . . ."

"Until what?"

"Well, one night I came home from work and Melanie greeted me at the door in a see-through negligee. The sight of her body drove me wild. I ripped off my clothes, hoisted her up in my arms, and forcibly carried her into the bedroom. I could tell by the look in her eyes that she was frightened and excited at the same time. Anyway, I couldn't have stopped myself if I wanted to—I was like an animal in heat, a wild beast in the throes of some instinctual force. I threw her down on the bed and tore off her negligee with a swipe of my nails. She had the greatest orgasm of her life. It must've lasted over an hour, wave after wave, again and again. As I reached orgasm myself, I started to bite and claw her with abandon. I couldn't control myself. The last thing I remember was plunging my teeth deep into her neck as I came and then passing out. When I woke up, she was dead."

"Oh my God," Younger Frank said. "And they didn't take into account the extenuating circumstances?"

"How could they? How could I ever explain what happened? I can hardly believe it myself. The prosecutor was convinced I had used a knife, and of course all the knives in our house had my fingerprints on them. They technically never found the murder weapon, but the circumstantial evidence was overwhelming. So I pleaded guilty because . . . because . . . I *am* guilty. But it's not my fault."

Older Frank pushed back on his cot and leaned against the cinder-block wall.

"Um . . . you're not still taking testosterone, are you?" Younger Frank asked.

"Oh, no. I went cold turkey before the trial so I could fit into my suit." He paused. "Anyway, you're cute, but not *that* cute."

Peccadilloes

"Y'all know how much I hate asking for money," Dr. R. James Blackwell stated from the pulpit of the First Baptist Church of Sugarville. "But the fiscal year ends in three days, and we're facing a shortfall of fifty thousand dollars in pledge fulfillments." It was a bright Sunday morning in late March and the sanctuary should have been packed, but Blackwell could detect holes in the congregation that wouldn't have been there a year earlier. Crossroads, the new nondenominational megachurch a few miles down the road, was clearly having a detrimental effect on his membership.

"The future of this church depends on the timely completion of the new Family Life Center," he continued. Although the land for the project had been donated by Miss Millicent Franklin through her last will and testament, Blackwell still needed his church members to ante up their fair share to fund the construction. "How can we have an effective community-outreach program without the proper facilities to hold Sunday school classes? There are grade-school children out there right now"—he pointed in the general direction of the parking lot—"*studying God's word in trailers.*"

He paused for effect, brushing down the lapels of his charcoal-gray Hart Schaffner & Marks suit and running a hand through his salt-and-pepper hair. A lone drop of perspiration fell from his nose and splashed on one of his immaculately polished Florsheim shoes.

"When the Lord commanded us to make disciples of all nations, he didn't intend for us to neglect our own backyard. No, we as Christians must proceed into the world from a position of strength, a position of confidence. That's why I'm asking you for your help, to make a sacrifice for the future of this church by fulfilling your pledges. Also, for those of you who haven't made a pledge yet, I'm setting aside this special offering for the building fund. Please look deep into your hearts, and even deeper into your wallets. And remember, the sacrifices we make here today could never equal the sacrifice Christ made for us on the cross."

He bowed his head and led the congregation in a long offertory prayer.

***

The Piccadilly Cafeteria was always crowded on Sunday afternoons, and today was no exception. Blackwell paid for his family and carried his tray to a small table his wife had secured in the middle of the dining hall. Just once he wished they could get there early enough to lay claim to one of those comfortable booths against the window, but after twenty years as a pastor he was becoming resigned to a fate of late lunches as the inevitable consequence of his profession.

Miriam and Elsa sat patiently waiting for him to say grace. He unloaded his dishes, removed his jacket, set his cell phone to vibrate, and sat down. Then, flipping his red power tie over his left shoulder, he took a quick sip of sweet tea and mumbled some pleasantries over the food.

"That was a . . . *nice* sermon, dear," Miriam said. She wore a smart blue dress with a dainty gold cross dangling from her neck. She'd recently had her hair cropped short and dyed a darker shade of auburn to make herself look younger.

"Sounded desperate to me," Elsa said, playing with her broccoli and cheese. She was a freckle-faced sixteen-year-old with silky red hair and emerald eyes. She wore a black sheath dress with a plunging neckline that prominently displayed her burgeoning breasts, and Blackwell had to avert his eyes to keep from connecting the dots on her chest.

"*Desperate?*" He nearly choked on his drumstick.

"Dad, you've been talking about money for weeks now. That's all you think about anymore. My friends even mentioned it in Sunday school—it's *embarrassing*."

"Listen here, young lady," he said, making a point with his drumstick. "Maybe if your *friends* got their parents to honor their commitments instead of buying them expensive cars, I wouldn't *have* to ask for money."

Miriam tugged on his sleeve. "Honey, don't take it out on Elsa. You did sound a little strident today."

"Oh, so now I was *strident*. That's just great." He dropped the drumstick on his plate.

"The Family Life Center is important," Miriam continued, "but it's not everything. It's not about how many people we can pack into the church, it's about reaching the people who *do* attend. A building never saved anybody—you know that. God will bring us more people if it's in His will. It's not about *quantity*, it's about *quality*."

"Tell that to the Southern Baptist Convention," Blackwell countered. "They're judging me on quantity *and* quality, and I've been sorely lacking in the *quantity* department lately. I'll never get a committee appointment if I can't keep my own flock under control. And *you*," he said, turning the spotlight of his anger back on Elsa, "I'm surprised you have any friends left—half of your so-called *friends* attend Crossroads now. That's where all the rich kids go to get their watered-down religion, isn't it?"

Elsa could have burned a hole in him with her eyes, but their conversation was cut short by the insistent buzz of his cell phone.

"Jim Blackwell," he answered, pasting a sudden smile on his face.

"Is this the *Reverend* R. James Blackwell?" asked the voice on the other end of the line.

"Yes, who is this?"

"Name's Jeremy Blunt. I believe we have a mutual friend in Millicent Franklin."

"Millicent Frank . . . oh, Miss Millicent. Yes, I know her— I mean, I *knew* her. She died about six months ago."

"I know. I'm her son."

Blackwell paused. "Her son? I wasn't aware—"

"I'm sure you weren't. I didn't attend the funeral. I'm calling because I'd like to set up an appointment with you."

"Um . . . sure. What's this all about?"

"I'd rather discuss it in person, if you don't mind. Your office, ten o'clock tomorrow morning?"

"Um, no, I have a staff meeting, then hospital duty in the afternoon. What about four o'clock?"

"Four o'clock it is. See you then."

Blackwell closed his cell phone and slumped down in the chair.

"You look like you saw a ghost," Miriam said.

He pushed his plate away. "Maybe I did."

***

Blackwell arrived at the church office at ten o'clock Monday morning after spending a restless night worrying about Blunt's phone call. The Miss Millicent he'd known had been an old maid who'd given up any thought of marriage or career early in life to take care of her widowed father. She'd been a longtime member of the church who'd preceded his ministry by some thirty years; compared to her, Blackwell was just another casual visitor. He'd presided over her funeral, but it had been a low-key affair attended only by elderly family members and a few close friends—no one under sixty, and certainly no children of her own. The very thought of Miss Millicent having a son was scandalous.

Blackwell went directly to the conference room where Stan Braxton, his minister of administration, had started the staff meeting without him. First on the agenda was the Sunday buzz, where the staff discussed the events of the previous day. But there was precious little to say as no one had been saved, no one had joined the church, and Blackwell's plea for money had fallen on deaf ears. That depressing news was followed by an interminable discussion of casual Fridays, a proposal Blackwell ultimately vetoed in favor of maintaining a professional image in the office at all times.

After the meeting, Blackwell took an early lunch at the Rexall with Buzz Parsons, a local congressman, before heading over to Gwinnett Medical in his blue LeSabre for hospital duty.

***

He returned to the church at three and cleaned up his office, adjusting the framed awards on his wall, dusting Elsa's Glamour Shots photo on his desk, and hiding next week's sermon from prying eyes. He normally wouldn't allow a complete stranger into the privacy of his inner sanctum—saving run-of-the-mill meetings for the business-like conference room—but he figured today might be a good day for a conscious display of power. He anxiously surfed the web while keeping an eagle eye out on the parking lot, which was barely visible from his office window if he twisted his head just so.

A silver Lexus sports coupe pulled up precisely at four, and a man in his early forties stepped out. He had slicked-back, jet-black hair and wore a smooth, charcoal-gray Armani suit and some kind of expensive Italian shoes. Blackwell watched as the man, presumably Blunt, removed his dark sunglasses, retrieved a thin metal briefcase from the cabin, and locked the car remotely behind his back.

Blackwell stared at the Lexus for a moment before heading to the front. He secretly wished he could afford a car like that, but tried to console himself with the knowledge he was setting a good example for his congregation by buying American. He wondered for the millionth time what his life would've been like if he'd earned an MBA instead of a ThD as he'd originally planned. He couldn't help but think he'd gotten his acronyms mixed up somewhere along the line.

Blackwell greeted Blunt in the foyer and promptly whisked him back into his office, closing the door behind them. He showed the younger man to a guest chair—a de-cidedly inferior position—then circled his desk and swooped down into his traditional executive brown-leather chair.

"So, Mr. Blunt, you claim you knew Miss Millicent?"

Blunt ignored him, instead focusing his attention on Elsa's photograph, which made her look more like a classy supermodel than a teenager in first blush. "Very nice," he said, more to himself than to Blackwell. Then he looked up. "Claim nothing—she's my mother. Look, I'm not much for chitchat. I'm more of a brass tacks kind of guy." He snapped open his briefcase and removed two legal documents, slapping them down on the desk.

"What's this?" Blackwell asked, backing away from the documents as if they were a pair of vipers. He fumbled for his glasses. "Are you a lawyer?"

"Nope, just a simple businessman. I own the Lexus dealership up at the Mall of Georgia. But let's stay on task, shall we? The document on your right contains the results of a maternity test I had performed. It proves beyond a shadow of a doubt that I'm Millicent Franklin's son. Let's just say I'm the product of a youthful indiscretion." A mischievous smile escaped his lips, making his black eyes sparkle. "But here's the real kicker. The document on your left is Millicent Franklin's will."

"Her *will*? She didn't leave a—"

"Not something you planned on, is it? Before you started tearing down my poor mother's house to build onto your church, I had all her papers shipped to my office. And, lo and behold, there among the useless receipts was this last will and testament—very official, with all the t's crossed and the i's dotted. You see, I have a pet theory. Call me cynical, but I think you coerced my dear old mother into signing away her property so you could build that architectural monstrosity over there." He pointed out the window at the Family Life Center. "I believe the technical term is *deathbed coercion*, but, as I say, I'm not a lawyer. Anyway, it turns out you don't own that property after all—I do. Isn't that a kick in the head?"

Blackwell grabbed the will off his desk and pored over it, but his hands were shaking so much he had to set it back down.

"Take your time, Jimbo. Of course, these are just copies. The originals are at the bank. Mom didn't believe in safety deposit boxes, but I do."

Blackwell started to sweat. "Oh my God," he whispered as he saw the name "Jeremy Blunt" featured prominently in the will.

"God has nothing to do with it," Blunt chuckled, "and I'm sure you'd like to keep the law out of it, too. I'd hate for it to become public knowledge that you took advantage of a little old lady on her deathbed. That would be simply criminal, wouldn't it? But I think we can settle this out of court, don't you? After all, we're both gentlemen."

Blackwell fell back in his chair. "What *do* you want? The building's almost complete."

"Oh, I don't want the property. With all due respect, this isn't a very nice neighborhood anymore."

"Money? Do you want money? The church is almost bankrupt, and I put my personal savings into the building fund."

"I don't want your money, either, though it's kind of you to offer."

"Then what do you want?"

"Well, we all have our little peccadilloes, don't we, Jimbo? Yours is deathbed coercion, and mine is . . ." He reached over the desk and turned Elsa's photograph to face him. "Very nice indeed," he said.

***

148

That night Blackwell couldn't sleep. He lay awake staring up at the stars in the ceiling's ersatz firmament, his thoughts flashing on and off like fireflies. Turning on his left side, he saw Miriam's face glowing like the moon in the radiance of the crucifix nightlight, the lines of merciless experience cratering around her eyes. Could this really be the same fresh-faced girl he'd chased around Southwestern Seminary like a rabbit in heat so many years ago?

One thing was perfectly clear—he'd made a strategic error by going to Miss Millicent's house alone. If only he'd thought to bring a witness with him. Of course, he'd been in the right in getting her to relinquish her property to the church. What did it matter to the old biddy anyway? Even her bastard son wasn't interested in that worthless piece of land. But if he'd only thought to bring a witness, perhaps an attorney from the church's law firm, he could have confidently strolled into court with testimony that she'd signed the document of her own free will. He had absolutely no doubt that, had she been of sound mind at the time, Miss Millicent eventually would have come to see his point of view. But now it was Blackwell's word against Blunt's, and Blunt had the upper hand. Court was not an option.

He turned over on his stomach.

"Stop flouncing," Miriam said.

"Sorry. Go back to sleep."

She draped an arm over his shoulder. "Are you all right?"

"I'm fine."

"No, you're not. You're sweating. Come over here."

She pulled his face down into her chest and gently stroked his hair, a sure sign of her amorous intentions. The last thing in the world he wanted right now was sex, but he felt the need to put up a good front to keep her from worrying, so he reached up and squeezed one of her breasts through the flannel nightgown. Still, he was far from getting an erection, and he had to think up something quick. Searching through his mind's catalog of erotic images, he settled on the familiar image of the church receptionist and soon was mounting Miriam in the missionary position.

***

The building dedication ceremony was held outside seven weeks later on a blustery Sunday morning in May. Blackwell had arranged for a dais to be set up over the steps of the Family Life Center, with a thousand folding chairs flowing out over the sidewalk and onto the lawn. The five ministers, all men, sat on the raised platform while the administrative staff, all women, sat below and to the left. Miriam, Elsa, and Buzz Parsons sat in the congregation in the front row, with the members of the building and finance committees sitting directly behind. The bulk of the folding chairs were jam-packed with church members decked out in their Sunday best.

The weather had held up for most of the morning, but as Blackwell stepped up to the microphone, a light drizzle began to fall and several umbrellas popped open. "Thank you for coming out today," he said as he watched a dark cloud bank bearing down on the church. "I'd especially like to thank Congressman Buzz Parsons for taking the time out of his busy schedule to be here." Parsons, a large man with a small toupee, stood and waved to the crowd as if he were addressing a huge political rally. Then he opened a green-and-white golf umbrella and sheltered Miriam and Elsa from the rain.

Blackwell soldiered on without protection as he saw lightning flash in the distance. "I'll keep my remarks short so we can go inside. I think we'd better postpone the prayer walk around the perimeter for later." He quickened his pace. "Three years ago when the building committee proposed the Family Life Center to the congregation, there were those among us who said First Baptist couldn't afford a state-of-the-art facility like this." He gestured to the drab rectangular structure with a sweep of his left arm; it looked more like a government office building than a place to harbor Christian souls. "Well, I'm here to tell you that not only have we completed the Family Life Center on time and within budget, but three days ago we paid off the loan to the Southern Baptist Convention. That's right—the Lord sent us an anonymous donor who helped us completely pay off this facility before the first Sunday school class was ever held!"

Several disparate "Amens" came from the crowd, but the applause was muffled by a steady downpour. Blackwell knew he had to get this over with soon. He bowed his head in prayer. "Lord, we thank you for bestowing this great blessing upon us. As stewards of your Word, we dedicate this Family Life Center to furthering the Gospel of Jesus Christ in the world. As it says in Timothy 2:19—" But in his haste Blackwell had forgotten the quote. He grabbed an index card from his suit pocket and read from it as the words blurred in the rain. "God's solid foundation stands firm, sealed with this inscription: 'The Lord knows those who are his.' Okay, let's go inside."

He didn't have to ask twice as the faithful rushed for the entrance.

"Let's have some lunch," Blackwell said as he tried to usher Parsons, Miriam, and Elsa into the building.

"Sorry, Dad, but I have to go to work now," Elsa said.

"Elsa got a job at a Lexus dealership," Miriam told Parsons.

"Congratulations!" Parsons responded cheerily.

Elsa gave Blackwell a quick peck on the cheek, ran through the rain to the parking lot, and hopped into her brand-new red Lexus IS300 SportCross.

Blackwell paused at the entrance to watch Elsa drive off, doubt clouding his thoughts for just a moment, but then he put his game face back on and walked confidently into the Family Life Center.

The Firing Squad

They marched us out to the courtyard at dawn and handed us preloaded M16s. There were four of us in the firing squad, but I was the only sharpshooter. Our commanding officer explained that one of the rifles contained blanks to ease our consciences, but I sincerely doubted they would be handing me a rifle with anything but live ammunition. I felt conflicted because all the men I had killed up until that point had clearly been enemy combatants, and I had no reason to believe this person was a bad guy.

They brought the prisoner out in an orange jumpsuit and shackles, a piece of paper affixed to his chest as a target. I was surprised and unnerved that he wasn't wearing a hood, which I had heard was customary for execution by firing squad. He appeared to be Arabic and in his midthirties, with short brown hair and a closely cropped beard, but what really bothered me was the calm acceptance in his eyes and the defiant rigidity of his posture. The only thing our commanding officer had told us about him was that he was out of his mind, but the man who stood before me now seemed anything but. Besides, if he really was out of his mind, didn't he need a psychiatrist more than a firing squad?

I had to take several deep breaths to keep my heart from racing, and I wiped a solitary bead of sweat from my brow before anyone could see it. They lined us up twenty feet from the prisoner, ordered us to raise our rifles, and commanded us to fire. I knew immediately that I had fired a live round and that I was the only one to hit the target. The other soldiers were good men but lousy shots. The prisoner slumped to the ground, and a few minutes later a doctor confirmed he was dead. There would be no plausible deniability for me.

Our commanding officer ordered us to bury the body outside the compound. Trading our rifles for shovels, we dragged the corpse into the forest and dug a six-foot-hole in the red Georgia clay. As we turned the body over to lower it into the hole, I noticed something was written on the paper target that I had missed before: "King of the Jews."

"Oh, no!" I said. "Not again!"

"What is it?" one of my buddies asked.

I tried to compose myself, but I was shaking uncontrollably. After a long pause, I said, "Never mind. It doesn't matter now."

We dumped the body in the hole and covered it up with clay.

I told the other men to go back without me and stood over the grave for a long time, hoping against hope for a miracle, but no miracle was forthcoming. In fact, there were only two things I knew for certain: he wasn't coming back again, and I would never forgive myself.

I walked back to the barracks alone.

The Man Upstairs

Harry Longview was exhausted after spending all day Friday helping his wife, Anna, settle into their brand-new Sugarville dream home. The movers had finished their work in the morning, so the two of them had spent the afternoon unpacking, putting up blinds, and taking trips to the home-improvement warehouse to meet the nearly insatiable demands of the enormous red-brick Colonial. There was plenty more to do in the house, but they still had the weekend ahead of them before having to pick up the kids at Grandmama's, so they took turns showering in the master bathroom, put on their summer pajamas, and met back at the king-size bed for couples devotional.

"Let's skip tonight," Anna said, hunkering down in bed.

Harry fixed her with a reproving glare. "We've never missed a night before."

"I know, but I'm tired."

"I'll keep it short."

Harry picked up his leather-bound Bible from the nightstand, turned to the next passage in their New Testament devotional, and read aloud: "Colossians 3:12–13. Since God chose you to be the holy people he loves, you must clothe yourselves with tenderhearted mercy, kindness, humility, gentleness, and patience. Make allowance for each other's faults, and forgive anyone who offends you. Remember, the Lord forgave you, so you must forgive others."

"Okay, I forgive you," Anna said, turning on her side.

"Forgive me? For what?"

"Everything."

After leading her in a short prayer thanking God for their new home and asking Him to watch over Harry Junior and Jenny, he laid his Bible down on the nightstand and turned off the light. They were both too excited to fall asleep right away, and way too tired for sex, so they talked for a while about the promise of their new lives in the Atlanta suburbs until Harry finally nodded off.

He was sleeping like a baby when Anna suddenly shook him awake.

"Did you hear that?" she said.

"Hear what?" He turned over and tried to go back to sleep.

She shook harder. "Harry!"

"What is it?" he said, becoming irritated.

"Somebody's *snoring*."

"Snoring? It's probably me."

"No, *listen*."

Now fully awake, Harry paid attention to the night: crickets chirping, a mournful train whistle in the distance, and *snoring*. Definitely snoring. It wasn't him, and it seemed to be coming from the attic directly above their bed. He looked at Anna's terrified expression in the moonlight and said, "Dial 9-1-1."

Jumping out of bed and turning the light back on, Harry rummaged through several unpacked boxes until he found his father's unloaded shotgun, which he had never fired but kept for the protection of his family. Marching into the hall, he flipped on the light switch to the attic, yanked down the folding wooden ladder, and ascended into the insufferable heat, his right calf still hurting from the day's labors.

To Harry's astonishment, there on a plywood platform in the middle of an ocean of pink insulation was a fully clothed, brown-skinned young man sleeping in the fetal position, snoring loudly, his head propped up on a filthy backpack. Harry wasn't sure what to do: confront the young man with an empty shotgun or go back downstairs and wait for the cops. Unfortunately, his decision was made for him when the noisy air-conditioner unit kicked on and the young man woke up, staring back at Harry from less than ten feet away. Harry raised the shotgun and pointed it at the young man, who, startled, sat up and lifted his empty hands in the universal gesture of surrender, pleading, "¡No me dispare!"

"Do you speak English?" Harry demanded.

"Sí, I mean yes. Please, don't shoot me."

Harry kept the shotgun trained on him anyway. "Who are you, and why are you in my attic?"

"My name is Jesús. I'm a construction worker. I helped build this house."

"Oh, I see," Harry said, lowering the shotgun slightly. "But why are you *sleeping* here?"

"I didn't know anyone had moved in. I'm working on another house down the block, and I've been staying here at night. I didn't have anywhere else to go."

"How did you get in? We've been here all day."

The young man pointed to a small hole beneath the eave with a tattered rope ladder bundled up beside it. Seeing it made Harry feel all the more violated and adamant about protecting his family.

"Well, somebody *has* moved in, and you're not welcome here. We'll just see what the police have to say about this."

With mention of the police, the young man became agitated and rose to his knees on the plywood platform. "Please don't call the police. I promise to leave and never come back."

"They're already on their way."

"But—but I don't have a green card."

"A green—? Oh, that's just great."

Harry raised the shotgun again. Nothing outraged him more than somebody who broke the rules. Harry had worked hard and played by the rules all his life, and now that he finally had something to show for it, he'd be damned if he let some two-bit illegal immigrant come into this country and take for free what he had earned through years of personal sacrifice. Unfortunately for the frightened young man, Harry held the unspoken belief that while New Testament forgiveness applied to him and his family, Old Testament justice applied to just about everyone else.

"Sit down right where you are and we'll wait for the police together."

But when a siren started wailing in the distance, the young man jumped up and sprang across the attic from joist to joist until he reached the opening, through which he began feeding the rope ladder. Harry, taken by surprise, yelled, "Stop!" and chased after him, but as he moved gingerly between the joists to avoid falling through the insulation, he experienced a painful charley horse in his right leg that made him trip and fall, causing the shotgun to go off with a deafening boom.

"Oh my God!" Harry said, stunned that it was loaded after all. Pushing himself back up to his feet, he saw the young man lying in a prone position under the eave with a gunshot wound in his stomach, bleeding profusely.

"Harry! Are you all right?" Anna called from downstairs.

"Yes, I'm fine. Don't come up here."

Harry negotiated the joists as best he could to reach the young man, only to realize there was nothing he could do.

"I'm so sorry," he said. "I—I didn't know it was loaded." The young man was writhing in pain, and Harry could only stand there helplessly and watch him suffer. "Hold on," he said. "The police are coming. They can help you."

As the moments ticked by and the blood drained from the young man's body, a kind of peaceful serenity came over his face, as if he knew he was going to die and was willing to accept it. The young man motioned for Harry to come closer. Harry kneeled down beside him, noticing for the first time that he wasn't much older than Harry Junior. The young man tried to muster a smile and said, "It's a beautiful house, no?"

Harry took the young man's calloused right hand in his own and looked into his eyes. "Yes," he said, "it's a very beautiful house. You did a good job."

"Thank you," the young man said, grimacing in pain. Then he whispered, "*Te perdono*," and died.

***

"It's not your fault," Anna said as they sat on the edge of the bed waiting for the police. "He shouldn't have been up there. It was self-defense."

"Self-defense," Harry parroted numbly.

As the sirens edged closer, Harry noticed a steady dripping noise coming from his nightstand and looked up to see a pool of blood forming on the ceiling. He rushed over to save his Bible but discovered the pages he'd been reading aloud were already covered with drops of blood. Pulling the nightstand out of the way, he grabbed an old T-shirt and tried wiping the bloodstains off, but he only succeeded in smearing the pages. He tossed the ruined Bible onto a stack of empty boxes and followed Anna downstairs to greet the police, repeating the phrase "self-defense" over and over in his mind like a prayer.

Watching the River Flow

T wo old friends sat on a park bench overlooking the Chattahoochee River in downtown Sugarville, watching the muddy water flow downstream just as it had for thousands of years before they were born.

"Did you hear the news?" Leon, a retired scientist, asked.

"What news?" Noel, a retired minister, answered.

"The probe! It finally reached the edge of the universe. They've already analyzed the data."

"So?" Noel was unimpressed.

"So?! They finished mapping the entire universe, that's all. And guess what? They found absolutely no evidence of God whatsoever. Zero, zilch, nada."

"That doesn't change anything."

"What do you mean? It changes *everything*. Without God as a crutch, maybe mankind will finally accept responsibility for his own existence, stop waiting for an afterlife that will never come, and try to make life right here on earth worth living." They'd been having this argument for what seemed like centuries, and Leon was fed up with Noel's intransigence.

"My life is already worth living, thank you very much," Noel said. "Anyway, we've been over this before. God is a supernatural entity. He's above reality, a metareality, if you will. *Of course* they didn't find any evidence of Him. They never will. So your so-called 'news' isn't going to change my beliefs one iota. But it might change yours."

"What do you mean?" Leon said.

"Look, Leon, you were an astrophysicist for what, thirty, forty years?"

"Uh-huh."

"And you spent a lot of time seeking physical evidence that humanity wasn't alone in the universe. First it was aliens, and then it was God."

"That wasn't my primary responsibility—"

"Yeah, but it was more than just a hobby. And you never found anything, did you?"

"Well, no," Leon admitted.

Noel faced Leon. "Then maybe you were looking in the wrong place. Instead of searching for meaning in outer space, maybe you should have been looking at *inner space* all along. During this century, science has proved there are no intelligent life-forms other than human beings, that man is physically alone in the universe. Do you really want to cut yourself off from God as well?"

Leon faced Noel. "Facts are facts. There's no such thing as a metareality. You might as well claim there's a bearded man in the sky. If there is a God, then He provided us with our minds for critical thinking and science as a tool for discovering Him. But since we didn't discover Him, it only follows that science was man-made and that God never existed."

Noel stood up. "Don't give me that bearded-man-in-the-sky crap! Your scientific beliefs require as much faith as my religious beliefs. The problem with you atheists is that you reject God, but you don't have anything to replace Him with—so you don't believe in anything. You're just a goddamned nihilist!"

Leon stood up. "I'm not a nihilist! The problem with you believers is that you adamantly refuse to change your beliefs in the face of new evidence, evidence that's right in front of your nose."

"Go to hell!"

"There *is* no hell!"

They started choking each other, and before they realized what was happening they stumbled down the embankment and fell into the river. Leon, who knew how to swim, hit his head on a rock and was knocked unconscious. Noel, who didn't know how to swim, simply disappeared beneath the water. They both drowned within seconds and were swept away by the current.

The muddy water continued to flow downstream as if they had never been there, just as it would for thousands of years after they were gone.

The Last Known Believer

M aximillian Stone was brushing his teeth late one night after getting home from the TV station when the angel Gabriel suddenly appeared in his bathroom, temporarily blinding him with magnificence and causing him to drop his toothbrush.

"Fear not!" Gabriel proclaimed.

"Who—who are you, and how did you get in here?"

"I am the angel Gabriel, messenger from the Lord God Almighty."

"Oh, that explains everything," Max said, shaking his head in disbelief. "Now I'm delusional."

Max's wife of fifteen years had recently divorced him for "being selfish," and he was having great difficulty adjusting to living alone. He had started seeing a psychiatrist who'd prescribed a powerful antidepressant that was known to have unusual side effects. This heavenly visitation must have been one of them.

He picked up the toothbrush from the tiled floor and gingerly placed it on the counter, his hand too unsteady to continue brushing. When he looked up, Gabriel was still there.

"You're not having a hallucination," Gabriel said. "I really *am* an angel, and I have a message for you from the Lord."

"But I'm an *atheist*."

"He's well aware of that. After all, He's omniscient."

"Then what could He possibly want from me?" Max spit out the toothpaste, rinsed his mouth out with water, and splashed his face for good measure. It didn't help.

"The Lord needs you to spread the word."

"What word—*insanity*? Jesus, I can't believe I'm having this conversation with myself."

"You're not making this any easier, Mr. Stone. Why don't you just take a couple of deep breaths and let me deliver the message, then you can decide for yourself."

"All right, all right," Max said, leaning against the counter for support.

Gabriel reached into the folds of his white linen robe and pulled out a parchment embossed with fine calligraphy. He read in mellifluous tones, "Maximilian Andrew Stone, I, the Lord God Almighty, Ruler of Heaven and Earth, am sending my messenger Gabriel to request your assistance in spreading the word about the Rapture—"

"Oh, for heaven's sake," Max interrupted, "the *Rapture*? I haven't believed in that old fairy tale since Sunday school. Who in his right mind would think that all the good Christians are going to be caught up in the air to meet Jesus while the rest of us poor bastards are left behind to undergo the tribulation? That's just plain silly."

"Let me finish," Gabriel said, his voice rising and his eyes flashing with anger. "Where was I . . .? Oh, yes—to request your assistance in spreading the word about the Rapture, which occurred last Tuesday night."

"What? It already happened? I didn't notice anything."

Gabriel looked up from the parchment. "Precisely. No one was taken."

"No one was taken?!"

"That's right. Jesus was there floating in the sky above Poughkeepsie waiting for his people to arrive, but nobody showed up."

"That's impossible! What about the billions of people who claim to be Christians?"

"Hypocrites, every last one. Believe you me, the Father, the Son, and the Holy Ghost were as surprised as anyone. I guess that's what happens when you give people free will—it can backfire big time. How do you think *Jesus* felt being stood up like a teenager on his first date? It was humiliating."

"But what does that have to do with me?"

"Our Lord is nothing if not patient, so He's decided to give humanity a second chance. After last week's debacle we got to thinking, if there aren't any authentic believers now, who's the last known believer we have on record? We had to do some serious data mining in the Book of Life to find out."

Max stared incredulously. "And the answer was *me*?"

"Yes."

"You've got to be kidding."

"Back in college, before you lost your faith in that world history class."

"Oh, yeah, I remember that. The professor showed us the similarities among the world's religions—similar creation myths, guy who comes back from the dead, afterlife, the whole enchilada. After that, I could never again claim that my religion was superior to anyone else's, and I eventually lost my faith."

"Of course they're similar," Gabriel said. "Religions are just a pale imitation of the truth, not the Truth Itself.

Humans are the ones who separate themselves into groups and call them religions, not God. Back then you were focusing on the intellectual problem of religion instead of simply having faith. You threw the Baby Jesus out with the bathwater."

"Wait a second—how did *you* know about my loss of faith?"

"I am the angel Gabriel, messenger from the Lord God Almighty."

"So I hear. This has to be the most persistent hallucination in history. Or—"

"Anyway, I'm not here to convert you. That's *your* problem. I'm here to get you to spread the word about the Second Rapture through your TV show."

"My TV show?" Max parroted. "So *that's* what this is all about. I should've known. You'll just have to speak to my agent."

"The Lord doesn't suffer intermediaries gladly. Haven't you heard of the Reformation?! You're a well-known cable TV personality, and millions of people around the world will listen to you. The Lord would like you to mention the Second Rapture on your news program tomorrow night. It's scheduled for next Tuesday at midnight in the sky above Poughkeepsie."

"But that doesn't make sense. You yourself just said religions are a pale imitation of the truth, but now you're talking about the fulfillment of a *Christian* prophecy."

"Well, some people will see Jesus, others will see Muhammad, and some might even see Gautama Buddha. Each person will perceive the archetype of God they've created in their own minds. God doesn't actually have a face, but if it makes you humans more comfortable to see Him wrapped in flesh, so be it. He works in mysterious ways, you know."

"So, let me get this straight: you want an atheistic anchorman to try to convince billions of unbelievers to show up in Poughkeepsie next Tuesday night for the Second Rapture."

"Think of it as a public service announcement."

"I'd rather think of it as professional suicide. Look, there are plenty of other anchormen that you could have asked to do this. Why me?"

"That's exactly what Moses said. The Lord felt that you're the perfect candidate because of your past faith and your current position. Frankly, you're our last hope. I don't mean to put undue pressure on you, but the salvation of billions of people depends on your answer. What shall I tell the Lord?"

"Let's assume for a minute that I'm not having a hallucination—that you're really Gabriel and God wants me to deliver this message to humanity. I have only one question."

"Yes?"

"What's in it for me?"

Gabriel's face glowed with anger and his body grew to an enormous height, filling the entire bathroom. But just when he looked like he was about to respond, he seemed to think better of it and vanished into thin air, leaving Max alone in his pajamas.

"Wow," he said to himself, "I can't wait to tell my shrink about this!"

Things Not Seen

Angela Roberts hated working at the lost-and-found desk in the Sugarville airport. She rarely helped anyone find anything, and as an aspiring actress she felt her time would be better spent auditioning for ingénue roles in downtown Atlanta. At thirty-two, her drama degree from Spelman, incredibly good looks, and light-skinned black complexion should have led her to leading lady roles in Hollywood by now, but her greatest triumph so far was a bit part in a racist musical at a local theater. Still, she needed to pay the rent, so she bought a skinny latte and a yogurt parfait from the airport coffee shop and settled in for another boring day in the boring suburbs.

She was just about to take another bite of strawberries when a dazed middle-aged white man in a rumpled raincoat wandered toward her.

"Can I help you?" she said, setting the plastic spoon down on the counter.

"Um . . . no, no thanks," he said, looking surprised someone had spoken to him. He was ashen faced, unshaved, and bedraggled, like he hadn't slept in days.

"Have you lost something?"

The man looked down at the "Lost and Found" sign for the first time. "I lost my wife," he whispered, more to himself than to her.

"Your wife? I can have her paged."

"No, you don't understand. She's *dead*."

"Dead?"

"Yes," he said, looking off in the distance. "She died in that . . . that plane crash."

"Oh my God," Angela said. She had been at the airport two days earlier when a small commuter jet had crashed in a beet field on approach, killing everyone on board. The NTSB still had the area cordoned off. "I'm so sorry."

"She was everything to me. I don't know how I'm going to raise those kids on my own. They're at her sister's house right now. The funeral's tomorrow at Sugarville Baptist, but I just keep coming back here . . . hoping . . ."

Angela had never seen anyone in such acute psychological distress before, and she felt powerless to help him. "Have you spoken to your minister?"

"My minister? What good would that do? He'd just try to fill me up with useless platitudes. He wouldn't be able to make any more sense of this than I can, because—because it just doesn't make any sense." He tapped on the sign. "That's another thing I'm losing, my faith."

Angela considered calling the airport psychologist, but she knew he didn't come in until nine. She decided that if anyone was going to help this poor man, it would have to be her.

"You know, my Great-Granny Anne was the most righteous Christian lady I've ever known," Angela said. "She led a very difficult life. She lost her son in Vietnam, and her husband committed suicide. But she remained optimistic her entire life. She used to say that 'everything happens for a reason.' We may not understand God's will at certain times during our lives, but God always knows the reason, and eventually we'll understand, if not in this lifetime then in the next, as long as we continue to have faith. I was very close to her, and when she died I felt like there was a gaping hole in my life. I still miss her dearly and think about her often, so I think I can understand what you're going through."

Angela picked up a framed cross-stitch that was lying on the counter, walked around the desk, and handed it to the man. "She gave this to me on her deathbed."

The man took the cross-stitch from her and read it aloud. "Faith is the evidence of things not seen."

"Great-Granny Anne never gave up on her faith, and neither should you."

The man started to choke up, then sobbed openly. Angela drew him to her and hugged him as he wept. "It'll be okay," she said.

After a few minutes, he stopped crying and seemed to remember something important, like he was waking up from a dream. "I have to get back to my children," he said, attempting to return the cross-stitch to Angela.

"You keep that," she said, "as a reminder."

"But it's your Great-Granny Anne's."

"I insist. She would want you to have it."

"Thanks," he said, placing the frame inside his raincoat. He wiped the tears from his eyes and headed toward the exit with a renewed sense of purpose.

Angela sat back down at her desk with a feeling of accomplishment. She had almost believed the story herself while she was "in the moment," and was certain her theater professors would have approved of her performance. She logged the silly cross-stitch that someone had dumped on her desk the previous day as "found" and returned to her yogurt parfait.

Maybe it was time to start auditioning for character parts.

The Holy Terror

The dead couple's funeral was held at Sugarville Baptist Church, but the internment was held later in the pouring rain at Oakland Cemetery in downtown Atlanta. Jonathan Godfrey, his wife, Melody, and his teenage daughter, Christine, stepped from their black Mercedes and huddled under a large golf umbrella, slogging behind the funeral director to the most ostentatious section of the cemetery. Perched on a hill, the Godfrey mausoleum looked like a miniature neo-Gothic cathedral replete with flying buttresses, pointed arches, and clerestory stained-glass windows, all topped by a large granite cross pointing the way to heaven. Built in the early 1880s by Jonathan's great-great-grandfather, the wealthy carpetbagger Heinrich Godfrey, it dwarfed most of the other mausoleums in the cemetery. Jonathan thought of it as the family's very own Tower of Babel, rising from the red Georgia clay in a hubristic attempt to touch the face of God.

Their minister, Dr. R. James Blackwell, was waiting for them in front of the mausoleum with Jonathan's father, Colonel Alexander Godfrey, his newly orphaned nephew, Bobby, and his father's blonde du jour, Liz, who had the unenviable task of looking after the fidgety ten-year-old. Blackwell assembled the small group at the base of the stairs, but with more people than umbrellas creating an awkward game of musical chairs in the rain, he was having trouble delivering the graveside prayer.

"Let's go inside," he said, climbing the marble steps and passing through the green-tarnished bronze doors without waiting for a response. Jonathan allowed his father, Bobby, and Liz to go first, then helped Melody and Christine negotiate the slick steps into the mausoleum. The funeral director remained outside with the umbrellas, standing like a sentry in the rain.

The columbarium was dark, dank, and cramped, with engraved memorials for several generations of Godfreys lining both walls. A crystal vase containing white lilies rested on a pedestal at the back, obscuring the original crypts of Heinrich Godfrey and his long-suffering wife, Martha. The memorials for his brother, Ron, and sister-in-law, Debbie, seemed almost out of place with their bright, white facades and newly chiseled nameplates.

Jonathan found himself inadvertently standing next to his father in front of his mother's memorial, but Blackwell interrupted them before they felt obliged to speak.

"Let's join hands," he said, catching Jonathan off guard. He quickly shifted positions to place Melody between himself and his father as they formed a lopsided circle in the middle of the room. Bobby, however, remained in front of his own mother's memorial, running his hand over the newly engraved letters.

"Bobby, come over here," the Colonel said, banging his cane on the floor like he was calling a dog. But Bobby seemed lost in thought and ignored him.

"That's all right," Blackwell said, leaving the boy to his own devices. "Let's pray."

The adults closed their eyes and bowed their heads as Blackwell led them in an excruciatingly long graveside prayer, rehashing many of the themes from the closed-casket funeral but embellishing them with a heightened sense of finality. Jonathan was surprised to hear Blackwell so effortlessly commend Ron and Debbie to heaven, especially when the two of them had discussed his brother's atheism on many occasions. In fact, Blackwell had never even met Ron or Debbie, and he certainly had no reason to believe they had lived good Christian lives. Yet, here he was, all evidence to the contrary, handing them first-class tickets to the Pearly Gates.

Blackwell, however, never got the chance to finish his prayer, as a loud crash ended it for him prematurely. Jonathan looked up to see the crystal vase lying in pieces on the floor, stargazer lilies scattered everywhere, and Bobby standing in a pool of water.

"I didn't do it!" Bobby shouted, but unless the ghost of Heinrich Godfrey had returned to cause the family further grief, there was no one else who *could* have done it.

"Bobby!" Liz yelled, rushing over to him and yanking him by the arm. That only made matters worse as Bobby started to screech like a caged animal, pulling away from her with all his might. When she steadfastly refused to let him go, he bit down hard on her forearm, drawing blood and forcing her to release him.

"*Jesus Christ!*" she screamed as Bobby raced out of the mausoleum.

"Go after him!" the Colonel commanded.

"*You* go after him," she said, nursing her injured forearm.

Jonathan considered running after the boy himself, but felt it wasn't his place to intervene. The colonel, meanwhile, stared Liz down, embarrassing her in front of the family.

She finally relented and stomped out of the mausoleum in a huff.

The funeral director appeared at the door. "Is everything—oh, my . . ." He rushed over to the shattered urn and picked up a jagged shard, examining it carefully in the faint light. "That's perfectly all right," he said. "I'll take care of it. Please, forget this ever happened."

***

The rain let up on the way back to the cars, and Jonathan's father surprised him by striking up a conversation. They hadn't spoken in three years.

"Could I have a word with you?"

"Um . . . yeah, I guess. What is it?"

"In *private*?"

Jonathan looked at Melody. "Go on," she said, waving him away.

The two of them paused in front of the bell tower, raindrops still dripping from the trees.

"I'm not interested in taking over Godfrey Homes," Jonathan said, making what he thought was a preemptive strike. "I don't want to get mixed up in the family business again."

His father scowled. "That's not what I wanted to talk to you about. Look, I'll get right to the point: Ron named me as the executor of his estate, but he named *you* as Bobby's legal guardian."

"He *what*?"

"In his will. If you had come to the reading, you would know that."

"I was busy—"

"Of course you were. Ron couldn't have known they would *both* die in that fire, but he did have the forethought to think of Bobby's future."

"Um, I'll have to talk to Melody about this."

"Naturally."

"I'm not committing to anything until I do."

"That's fine. You do what you have to do, but there's really no other choice. It's either that or he goes to a foster home. I'm too old to raise a kid, especially a holy terror like that."

"But you're not too old to screw a thirty-year-old?"

The colonel's face reddened. "Whatever." He pulled a document out of his coat pocket and handed it to Jonathan. "Here's the will. Think of it as a subpoena. You've been served."

***

Because there really *was* no other choice, and because he and Melody agreed it was "the Christian thing to do," Jonathan initiated the adoption process and brought Bobby home for dinner the following Wednesday. The four family members sat down at an informal kitchen table covered by a red-and-white-checkered tablecloth. Melody had prepared a welcoming dinner of fried chicken, mashed potatoes with white gravy, fried okra, cornbread, and sweet tea. Steam rose from the plates like an early-morning fog hovering over the Chattahoochee.

Jonathan sat down in the captain's chair as Melody passed the cornbread to Bobby, who promptly grabbed a piece and stuffed it into his mouth.

"Not yet," Melody whispered, gently restraining the boy. Bobby looked surprised but placed what was left of the cornbread down on his plate.

Raised by wolves, Jonathan thought.

"Pass the basket," Melody prompted, and Bobby handed the cornbread to Christine.

After everyone was served, Melody said, "Honey, would you say the blessing?"

"Sure," Jonathan said, happy to demonstrate to the boy how civilized people behaved. "Let's pray." He bowed his head but delayed closing his eyes for a moment to see if Bobby would follow his lead—which, of course, he didn't.

"Heavenly father," Jonathan said, "we come to you under difficult circumstances, but we thank you for bringing this new family together. Lord, bless Bobby as he begins a new life with us, and help us provide a good example for him to follow. Bless this food to nourish our bodies, and keep us ever mindful that the nourishment of our hearts and minds only comes from your word. We ask these things in Jesus's name. Amen."

Jonathan opened his eyes to see Bobby still staring at him as if he were an alien creature.

"Amen," Melody said. "Let's eat."

After dinner, Jonathan brought up the last member of the family from the basement to introduce him to Bobby. Unfortunately, no one had asked Bailey the beagle if he wanted a new companion, and apparently he didn't. He ran straight for Bobby and stood three feet away from him, barking. Jonathan had never seen the dog so agitated before, and when his bark turned into a growl and then into a snarl, he finally had to carry Bailey back down to the basement without a proper introduction.

When Jonathan returned to the table, Christine had taken Bobby upstairs to show him his room.

Melody said, "Did you see his eyes?"

"Whose eyes?"

"Bobby's. They were *black*."

***

In an ongoing attempt to civilize the boy, Jonathan and Melody took Bobby to the eleven o'clock service on Sunday at Sugarville Baptist Church. Christine drove separately to attend Sunday school with her friends and sat as far away from them as possible during the service. Blackwell seemed much more at ease on his home turf than at the internment, his preternaturally white smile shining down from the pulpit like a beacon. Bobby fidgeted between them in the pew, but settled down to draw when Melody handed him the program and a pencil.

As a deacon, Jonathan was responsible for helping to pass the offertory plates before the youth minister delivered the children's sermon. When Blackwell gave the signal, he and five other men stood up, solemnly walked to the front in their suits and ties, and followed the preordained procedure of passing and accepting the plates from the congregation. His own offering was debited from his checking account on the fifteenth of every month, so there was no reason for him to contribute now. In fact, fewer and fewer people contributed physical checks or cash anymore, but Blackwell insisted on performing the dead ritual just in case a visitor felt particularly generous.

When Jonathan returned to the pew, Melody nudged Bobby toward the front of the sanctuary to be with the other children. As he half listened to the children's sermon—something about God being more powerful than all the evil in the world—Jonathan glanced down at what Bobby had been drawing and, shocked, picked it up to look closer. It was a convincing portrait of Blackwell as a winged demon hovering in the air, blood dripping from his fangs.

Jonathan leaned over to show Melody.

"It's just the grief," she said.

***

Grief or not, Jonathan and Melody soon realized they were in over their heads. The boy needed professional help. Jonathan obtained the name of a child psychologist from Blackwell on Monday morning and arranged an appointment for later in the week.

That night after dinner, he poured himself a tall glass of sweet tea, grabbed his tablet computer, and headed for the screened-in deck at the back of the house. Now that summer was over and fall imminent, he knew he wouldn't have many more such opportunities to relax outdoors, and after a busy day analyzing annual reports he looked forward to a little peace and quiet. As he sat down in his favorite chaise lounge and sipped tea, he took in a spectacular view of the Chattahoochee River in the fading light of day.

But his reverie was broken when the neighbors' children ran laughing between the houses and made a beeline for their own backyard. You'd think with all the money he'd paid for this house, a little privacy would've come with the bargain, but the Kendricks' postage-stamp yard was nearly on top of his own, and privacy fences were disallowed by the homeowners association.

As Franky and Brooke sprinted toward the giant oak supporting their custom-made treehouse, Jonathan was surprised to see Bobby and Bailey emerge from the other side of the house to meet up with them at the base of the tree. Even more surprising was the fact that Bailey was off his blue leash—something he'd discussed with Bobby only that morning. Not wanting to embarrass the boy by scolding him in front of his new friends, Jonathan laid the tablet down on his lap and watched the children from a discreet distance.

"Let's go up," Franky said, grabbing the first rung of the sturdy wooden ladder. He was a lanky blonde boy, a full head taller than Bobby.

"What about Bailey?" Brooke said, playing with the pink ribbon in her shiny brunette hair.

"Leave him here," Franky said, already starting to climb. "Come on!"

"We can't do that!" she said, leaning down to chuck the beagle's chin, his brown-and-white tail wagging amiably in response. "Why don't you and Bobby go up. I'll stay down here with Bailey."

"Suit yourself," Franky said, already halfway up the tree.

Without warning, Bobby picked up Bailey, carried him over to the tree, and followed Franky up the thirty-foot ladder, holding the dog in one hand while grasping the rungs with the other.

Jonathan jumped up and rushed to the screen door, but by the time he uttered a feeble "hey," Bobby and Bailey had already disappeared into the treehouse. He stood there helplessly for a moment, pushing and releasing the door, torn between the desire to protect his dog and the reluctance to interfere with the children's fun. Ultimately, as he watched little Brooke scamper up the ladder after the boys, he resolved to leave the children alone and returned to the chaise lounge and his tablet.

He was almost finished reading an article on the drought in Georgia when he heard a loud thud followed by a girl's scream. Looking up, he saw Bailey lying on his side, motionless beside the trunk of the giant oak.

Throwing down the tablet and bursting through the screen door, Jonathan ran as fast as he could to the Kendricks' backyard, reaching Bailey just as the children scurried down the ladder. He kneeled down to place his hand on Bailey's chest—thankfully, the dog was still alive. He looked up at the children. "*What the hell happened?*"

The three of them looked back and forth at each other several times, then Franky spoke. "Bobby—"

"He *fell*," Bobby said, staring at Franky.

"Um . . . yeah," Franky said, kicking an exposed tree root with his sneaker. "He fell."

"But—" Brooke said.

"*He fell*," Franky repeated, grabbing Brooke's arm.

Luckily, Bailey had plunged into a thick patch of uncut grass and looked more stunned than hurt. He got up slowly on his own, shaking off the blow and wobbling over to stand behind Jonathan, whimpering quietly to himself.

Jonathan stood up. "Well, I guess he's okay, but you really need to be more careful. No more dogs up in the treehouse, understood?"

"Yes, sir," Franky said.

"And where's his leash?" Jonathan said, looking at Bobby.

"Um," Bobby said. "Back at the house."

Franky and Brooke excused themselves, racing home like two prisoners escaping the penitentiary. Jonathan and Bobby walked back to the house together, Jonathan cradling Bailey in his arms.

"What did I tell you about keeping Bailey on his leash?" Jonathan said.

Bobby ignored him, instead pulling a black pocket lighter out of his jeans and flicking it on and off.

"Give me that!" Jonathan said, taking the lighter. "*What did I tell you about the leash?*"

"What's the big deal?" Bobby said, taking off at a breakneck pace for the house.

"Hey! I'm talking to you!" Jonathan shouted, but his words were swallowed up by the deepening night.

***

Jonathan left work early on Thursday afternoon to meet Melody and Bobby at the child psychologist's office in downtown Sugarville. Laura Bennett was a short, middle-aged woman with a relaxed demeanor who shared an office with two other psychologists. The only distinguishing feature of the otherwise nondescript space was a playroom for children off to the side of the waiting room.

After the initial consultation with the three of them—which included answering a detailed checklist and questioning the boy directly while he alternately fidgeted or stared off into space—Laura excused Bobby to go to the playroom while she talked to Jonathan and Melody alone.

"I'm concerned," she said, closing the door behind her. She sat down on the matching love seat opposite theirs. "Bobby is demonstrating the classic symptoms of reactive attachment disorder. I've seen this with adopted children before, but nothing to this level. What can you tell me about his biological parents?"

"Well," Jonathan said, glancing at Melody, "my brother and I had a falling out about three years ago . . ."

"A falling out? What happened, if you don't mind my asking?"

"Oh, no, that's fine. I was the CFO of Godfrey Homes for ten years, but when my father and brother tried to get me to inflate our earnings, I refused to do it and left the company. We haven't had much contact with Ron or Debbie since then, so I really couldn't speak to their parenting skills."

"That's not entirely true, Jonathan," Melody said. "We saw plenty of their so-called 'parenting skills' on display before we broke off contact with them. Ron was an alcoholic—"

"Honey—"

"Jonathan, if we're going to help Bobby, we need to be completely honest. Ron was an alcoholic and Debbie was a social climber. I'm pretty sure Bobby was an accident, and they didn't spend much time with him at all. In fact, they hired a live-in au pair specifically so they could spend even *less* time with him."

Jonathan nodded in agreement.

"I see," Laura said. "Did you ever see any evidence of physical violence?"

"No," Melody said. "Not that I can remember."

"Or sexual abuse?"

"Oh, no, nothing like that. I just think Bobby grew up in an environment of benign neglect."

"Neglect is never benign," Laura said, taking a deep breath. "I'm going to recommend a two-part strategy. First, I'd like to see Bobby one on one on a weekly basis for a while. I can't say for exactly how long—it all depends on how he responds to the treatment. My initial goal will be to establish trust, which is a prerequisite to the actual therapy, and that could take some time."

Jonathan looked at Melody for approval. "Okay," he said. "That's fine."

"Second, and this may be a little controversial for you, I'm going to recommend something called attachment therapy. Have you ever heard of it?"

"No," they said in unison.

"Attachment therapy is where the adoptive parents take an active role in the treatment. You would physically hold Bobby down until he stops resisting you, and then you would force him to establish eye contact with you. It's something you would only do in my office and under my supervision. I'm a licensed practitioner."

"Is that really necessary?" Jonathan said.

"Yes, I think it is. Look, you don't have to commit to this right away. I'll start with the one-on-one therapy first. It's a personal decision, and it depends on how serious you are about integrating the boy into your family. I'll provide you with some information on attachment therapy before you go. Just think about it."

"Yes, of course," Melody said, "We'll talk it over."

187

Laura escorted them to the playroom, where Bobby sat in the middle of a pile of broken toys holding a decapitated baby doll.

***

Jonathan and Melody invited Blackwell and his wife, Betty, over for dinner the following Tuesday. With Christine sleeping over at a friend's house, Jonathan put Bailey in the basement before dinner and sent Bobby to his room to watch TV after dinner so the adults could speak alone.

"So you saw the therapist I recommended?" Blackwell asked, taking a seat on a brown-leather couch in the great room.

"Yes," Jonathan said, "and she was very helpful. She's going to see Bobby on a weekly basis for the foreseeable future."

"Good. Laura has helped a number of adoptive parents I've sent her way. And she's a *Christian* therapist, so she has sound beliefs as well as a solid background in the latest therapies."

"Well, that's what we wanted to talk to you about. Melody and I have been praying and talking about a therapy that Laura recommended. But we need your advice."

"It's called *attachment therapy*," Melody said. "Have you heard of it?"

"Yes, in fact I have. Laura and I discussed it on several occasions, and I've seen it work for adoptive families before. Church members, even, though of course I can't say who. Anyway, Laura has my complete confidence."

"Isn't it a bit . . . extreme?" Melody said.

"I understand your reservations, but some children, especially boys, need an added layer of discipline to help them integrate into a new family. In any case, you might only need a few sessions to see positive results. I've seen some remarkable results even after only one session. It might be just the thing to help you bond with Bobby. You could think of it as laying on of hands, a practice that goes back to the Old Testament."

"I'm more of a New Testament girl myself," Melody said. "You know, love, forgiveness—"

"Melody has a point," Betty said. "You men always want to resort to force, and look at the mess the world is in because of it."

Blackwell scowled. "Laura is a woman, and she believes in attachment therapy. Look, I can't make this decision for you, you're going to have to make it by yourselves. All I can say is you have to let God be the tiebreaker. You have my complete support whatever you decide to do."

***

A half hour later Blackwell asked to see Jonathan's deck and immediately lit up a cigarette. A full moon hovering over the Chattahoochee made the pine trees appear in silhouette.

"I thought you gave those up," Jonathan said.

"I did. In fact, I've been giving them up for thirty years. There's a debate in my head going on about it all the time."

"Maybe you should let God be the tiebreaker."

Blackwell smiled. "Touché." He took another drag. "Look, Jonathan, are you really prepared for this? Attachment therapy can be brutal, not just on Bobby but on you. The father typically takes the lead because he's the strongest, but it's not just the physical aspect, it's the mental. You have to persevere through the sessions. You can't hold back. Have you seen the videos?"

"There are *videos*?"

"Oh, yeah. I'll send you some links."

"I'm worried about it, but Laura seems to think it's necessary. I'm not expecting miracles."

Blackwell exhaled a thick cloud of smoke into the night air. "Miracles are all around us, Jonathan. We only have to open our eyes to see—*what's that?*"

"What's what?" Jonathan looked to where Blackwell was pointing, but he couldn't see a thing in the dark.

"Do you have a flashlight?" Blackwell said.

Jonathan grabbed a large flashlight from a nearby table, handed it to Blackwell, and followed him down to the river. "Be careful," he said, "there are snakes down here."

Blackwell marched to a large oak tree next to the river and pointed the flashlight up into the branches. Hanging from a high branch by his blue leash was Bailey, motionless.

"*Jesus Christ!*" Blackwell said, climbing the tree to cut the dead dog down. Jonathan, in shock and disbelief, helped Blackwell lower Bailey to the ground, confirmed he was dead, and whispered one word: "Bobby." Jumping up, he ran back into the house.

"Where is he?" he asked Melody.

"In his room. What's the matter?"

Jonathan ran up the stairs and burst into Bobby's bedroom, but the boy was curled up in his bed in his pajamas with the TV turned down, sleeping like a baby. He hesitated on the threshold for a moment—anger pushing him forward, doubt pulling him back—until Melody came up from behind him and convinced him to return to the den.

After explaining what they had found to Melody and Betty, Jonathan and Blackwell returned to the backyard and buried Bailey by the light of the moon. After the Blackwells left, Jonathan called Laura to arrange an attachment-therapy session for the next morning and then, locking the master-bedroom door behind him, huddled on the bed with Melody in the dark, exchanging whispers.

***

Jonathan and Melody, not having slept much the previous evening, took Bobby to Laura's office early the next morning without telling him why they were going. Laura, who had shuffled her schedule to meet with them, greeted them in the waiting room and ushered them into her office. Bobby sat down on one love seat, Jonathan and Melody sat down on the other, and Laura placed a ladder-back chair in the middle and sat down there.

"Now, Bobby," Laura started, "we're going to try something new today. First, I'm going to ask your parents—"

"*Adoptive* parents," Bobby said.

"Yes, of course, your *adoptive* parents. I'm going to ask them to sit by you."

"Why?" Bobby said, but Jonathan and Melody moved over to bookend him like they had previously discussed with Laura on the phone.

"Good," Laura said, looking at Jonathan and Melody. "Now, I want each of you to take one of Bobby's arms."

"What?" Bobby said.

They each grabbed an arm and held him against the back of the couch.

"What are you doing?" Bobby said.

"How do you feel, Bobby?" Laura asked.

"I feel . . . uncomfortable. Let me go!"

But they continued to hold him. In fact, they held him even tighter as he started to struggle.

"Now, Bobby," Laura said, "your adoptive father has a few questions he'd like to ask you."

Jonathan tried to make eye contact with Bobby, but Bobby continued to fidget and look away.

"Bobby," he said as calmly as he could under the circumstances, "I want you to be completely honest with me. What did you do after dinner last night?"

Bobby finally answered, "I went upstairs and watched TV, like you told me."

Now he was trying to escape, but the more he struggled, the more they held him down. Melody started holding him from behind while Jonathan held him down by his chest. The boy was facing him but still looking away, and Jonathan was getting impatient. "Did you leave your bedroom for any reason?"

"No. What are you—stop it!"

"Did you go outside with Bailey?"

"No! Let go of me!" Bobby flailed his arms and legs, and Melody had trouble holding him still. Jonathan redoubled his effort, pushing down on the boy's chest, his face turning red and his breath getting heavier with the exertion.

"Did you kill Bailey?" Jonathan said, unable to maintain the calm and cool that Laura had recommended.

No answer.

"Did you *kill* Bailey?" he repeated, moving up Bobby's chest to his neck.

No answer.

"*Did you kill Bailey?*" he shouted, starting to strangle the boy.

Now Bobby couldn't have answered even if he wanted to.

Melody let go of Bobby's arms and shouted, "*Jonathan!*"

Jonathan suddenly realized what he was doing and let go. The boy coughed twice to start breathing again, then jumped up and ran out of the office, Laura fast on his heels.

"I'm—I'm sorry," Jonathan said, shaking his head. "I don't know what got into me."

Laura returned a few minutes later and said, "He's gone."

***

Three days later Bobby was still gone, and Jonathan felt terrible. After filing a missing person's report with the police, he took the rest of the week off and, sleeping and eating very little, spent the daylight hours aimlessly driving around Sugarville searching for the boy. Before the attachment-therapy session, he'd been sure that Bobby had murdered Bailey, but the boy's steadfast denial in the face of intense pressure made him doubt his earlier conviction. Now he was facing the possibility that he'd been wrong all along, and he felt increasingly responsible for anything that might happen to Bobby. A ten-year-old boy wandering around the Atlanta suburbs by himself faced a multitude of dangers, and if Bobby came to any harm on his watch, Jonathan could never forgive himself.

Passing by the old Sugarville courthouse for the umpteenth time, Jonathan decided to expand his search area by driving to his brother's house in unincorporated Sugarville. Although the second floor had been destroyed by fire, the bricked-in first floor was still intact and might provide a temporary hiding place for a resourceful young man. It was a long shot because his brother's house was at least five miles from Laura's office, but he thought it would be a mistake to underestimate the boy. Besides, he had run out of other ideas and didn't want to go home to Melody empty handed for the third day in a row.

He reached Ron and Debbie's old subdivision as the sun began its final descent in the west. Fortunately, he remembered the keypad code to enter the gated community, and the black wrought-iron fence swung inward to admit his Mercedes. He navigated a maze of McMansions that put the size of his own house to shame until he found the biggest house in the subdivision, strategically positioned at the end of a cul de sac. Nothing was too ostentatious for Ron and Debbie.

He parked his car on the empty street and got out to look around. There were blue tarps covering the roof and black soot stains on the exterior brick, but no obvious signs of recent activity. He ascended the steep and winding driveway to the garage but knew right away from the smoke damage that no one could possibly inhabit this side of the house. He followed the sidewalk around to the front door and pushed it open, but the smoke and water damage there made the downstairs uninhabitable as well.

Dejected, he closed the front door and trudged back down to his car. However, as he was unlocking the driver side door, a glint of light from a nearby storm drain caught his attention. Kneeling down to get a better look, he saw a small object lodged in the matted pine straw and reached in to pull it out. It was a black lighter exactly like the one he'd taken away from Bobby. At first he thought maybe Bobby had been here after all, but Jonathan had locked up that lighter in the desk drawer of his home office, and there was no way Bobby could have gotten it back. This had to be a second lighter. Jonathan looked up at the house and down at the lighter several times, then stood up and, steadying himself from a sudden dizziness, jumped in his car and raced out of the subdivision.

***

Jonathan ran three red lights frantically driving home in the dark, but when he reached his house it was already engulfed in flames. Jumping out of the car with the motor still running, he burst through the front door into the great room but was met by a cloud of black smoke.

"Melody! Christine!" he shouted, but there was no answer.

Coughing several times, he ripped off his polo shirt and held it over his mouth as he ran up the stairs two at a time. He found Melody on the second-floor landing in front of Christine's bedroom door, collapsed and unresponsive. He checked her pulse but found none.

"*Jesus Christ!*" he cried.

The door knob was hot to the touch, so he wrapped his shirt around his hand and tried to open it that way. Locked. He kicked the doorjamb several times before it gave way, but he was blown back by a wall of flames and fell to the ground. He got up and ran into the room to find Christine unconscious in front of a slightly cracked window. Fighting the flames, he picked her up and carried her downstairs, vowing to return for Melody. The path to the front door was now blocked by flames, so he carried Christine out the back and lowered her to the ground, her pulse weak and breathing shallow.

He ran back into the great room, but he caught fire before he could reach the stairs. Panicking, he rushed outside and rolled around in the grass until the flames were extinguished. Realizing that Melody was already dead and that he couldn't help his daughter by putting himself in further jeopardy, Jonathan returned to Christine and started administering CPR. But after several minutes of compressions and breaths, he realized she, too, was dead. He sat on the cold, hard ground hugging her lifeless body and began to sob.

As he sat there watching his house evaporate into the air and listening to the approaching sirens, he heard a twig snap behind him and realized he wasn't alone. Jumping to his feet, he saw the silhouette of a boy standing beneath the tree where Bailey had been murdered and knew instantly that it was Bobby. Overcome by rage, he ran toward the boy, but Bobby waded into the Chattahoochee and started slogging to the other side. Jonathan followed him into the river and, overtaking him in the middle, thrust Bobby under the water and held him down like he was baptizing the boy. But Jonathan was weak from his ordeal and couldn't hold Bobby for long. When the boy popped back up out of the water and pushed him away, Jonathan slipped on a rock, fell into the river, and swallowed a lungful of water. Unable to save himself, he floated downstream to the deepest part of the river and started to drown. The last thing Jonathan saw was the image of Bobby standing on the opposite bank of the river, smiling.

About the Author

J.J. Haas's short stories have appeared in *Shenandoah*, *Baen's Universe*, and *The Literary Hatchet*, and his poetry has appeared in *Rattle Magazine*, *Writer's Digest*, *The Magazine of Fantasy and Science Fiction*, and *Asimov's Science Fiction*. He is a senior content developer for a Fortune 500 company and a Fellow of the Society for Technical Communication, where he received the Distinguished Chapter Service Award and led the Atlanta chapter to the Chapter Achievement Award as president. As an alumnus of the University of Chicago, he is the president of the alumni club of Atlanta, leading that organization to the inaugural Alumni Club of the Year Award. He lives in a northeast suburb of Atlanta with his wife, Melissa, and two West Highland white terriers.